Sorceress
of the
Himalayas

Sorceress of the Himalayas

KETAKI SHRIRAM

CRYSTALLIUS PRESS
Menlo Park, California

Crystallius Press
2725 Sand Hill Road, Suite 120
Menlo Park, CA 94025
www.crystalliuspress.com
www.sorceressofthehimalayas.com

ISBN: 978-0-615-19841-5

Designed and Printed by *the*BookDesigners
www.bookdesigners.com

Printed in China

10 9 8 7 6 5 4 3 2

Contents

Foreword by Catherine Head   ix

Prologue: The Pariah   1

An Untimely Passing   29

A New Friend—And a Guide   49

The Golden Pass   59

Daya   67

A Sign of Evil   71

The Grove   82

Disunity   85

The Dark Rider   91

Into the Village   99

The Passing of Sangmu   104

Chased by Shadows   115

Reading Rinzen   121

Encountering the Dragon King   130

The Ruler of the Ghost Monastery   138

The Steps of Death   142

The Crystal River   164

The Shapeshifter's Betrayal   176

A Duel in the Monastery   180

The Sacred Forest   186

Revelations   196

A Fight for Power   200

The Hidden Castle   207

Stories Pieced Together   217

In the Garden   220

The Enchanted Well   228

The Dungeon   234

Austin's Redemption   237

A Promise   241

The Final Sacrifice   244

Joy Within Sadness   253

The End Begins   258

Epilogue: Reunited   262

Acknowledgments   267

About the Author   268

Foreword

Against a backdrop of the majestic Himalayas, Ketaki Shriram's first novel moves from its fairy tale beginning to quickly envelop us in a world of believable magic. It is both a realistic world where parents debate children's needs, where racial prejudice corrupts loving relationships, where loved ones die, and a magical world where a ratty brown leather book with "several rips that had been hastily mended with thin white thread" holds the key to human and magical lives. It is also a world where a young woman chooses to follow her father's sorcerer path, defying the traditions that say she must marry as her father wishes. Her forbidden love starts a saga covering generations and examining the real meaning and power of love, as her mixed-race daughter seeks the family she has never known and the book of magical spells.

Tien is accompanied on her quest by a band of magical creatures, each with its own reasons for seeking the book, and each hiding secrets that will ultimately save the world or leave it in the clutches of the dark Force forever.

Ketaki Shriram here joins the ranks of writers in the finest tradition of fantasy fiction, creating a story appealing on the personal level to anyone who has felt like an outcast, and enthralling in its sweeping creation of a world threatened by best intentions gone awry.

Ironically, Ketaki is a student for whom little goes wrong. *Sorceress of the Himalayas* was written when she was just thirteen; she decided soon thereafter that she would have her work published and sought me out for help in achieving those ends. Alas, I knew next to nothing about publication, but I was able to direct her to my colleague, Kerry Mohnike, who introduced Ketaki to the complex and often defeating world of finding a publisher. Ketaki has taken it from there on her own, much as Tien accepted the quest she was given and persisted despite the obstacles in her way. Confident and cheerfully determined, Ketaki makes sure she finds a path leading to her goals.

Now a junior in high school, Ketaki is revising her second novel, one very different from the world and the concerns of the Himalayan Tien, but nonetheless familiar in theme: the strength of women and the wrongs of racial discrimination. As we work together hammering out plot and motives, I find myself consistently impressed by both Ketaki's clear vision of her world and characters and her willingness to adjust that vision as she grows as a writer and refines her skills. I have no doubt that Ketaki Shriram, should she continue to pursue this path, soon will be a presence on bookshelves across the country.

—Catherine S. Head | FEBRUARY 2008

Sorceress
of the
Himalayas

Prologue

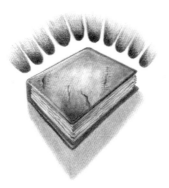

The Pariah

The old wooden door creaked and shuddered as the man banged against it with his large pitchfork. He waited for several moments after the loud knock, but the house behind the door remained dark and silent, bathed only by the silvery light of the stars.

"Kamsa, you old fool! We know you are hiding." The man stepped back once more, and motioned with his free hand. Another man standing behind him, this one brandishing a sword, handed the first man an oil lantern. Holding the bright light up, the leader of the group banged on the door a second time.

It creaked open. Peering inside, the leader was able to

see the stooped and weary figure of a man in the gloom of the tiny hut.

"What is it you want?" Kamsa did not move into the light of the lantern as he spoke; instead, he seemed to cringe at the sight of the bright flame.

"To speak with you." The leader's tone was brusque and filled with contempt. Kamsa made to close the door, but the leader stabbed his pitchfork into the rotting wood, the forked steel spikes glimmering under the light from the lantern.

Kamsa appeared unconcerned by this violent action. Calmly stepping forward into the light, he steadily gripped the pitchfork and pulled it out of the door. Three holes remained. Kamsa frowned when he saw these, and turned his dark eyes toward the men. They shuffled backwards hurriedly, as though afraid of the man before them.

"What is it you wish to speak about?" His voice was quiet, but tight with irritation.

"Do not be impatient with us," snarled the burly leader of the men, who was quickly regaining his confidence. "We have come to speak with you of the incident that occurred at your home last night."

"What incident?" Kamsa's eyes bore into the burly man's lighter ones. He faltered for a moment, then blustered, "The-I-you know what we mean!"

The other men shouted their agreement, their calls and cries echoing throughout the silent village.

"You will wake your wives and children," said Kamsa to the men.

"We know what happened here last night!" Another man, of considerably less size but more intelligence, stepped forward.

"It was dark magic," said the leader. A long silence fell. Kamsa looked from man to man, the corners of his mouth twitching. When none of his fellow villagers smiled, Kamsa asked incredulously, "You truly believe I am dabbling in dark magic?"

"What else could explain why you stay in your home all the time? You have no other jobs to speak of, and your physique has changed so much!" The smaller man piped up once more, eyeing Kamsa's lined, weary face thoughtfully.

Touching his face with his hand, Kamsa said softly, "This is not the result of dark magic...it is..."

But what it truly was, he could not be brought to say. The men waited for several moments before the leader spoke once more.

"You must leave. This has gone too far. We will no longer stand for your strange magical dabbling, dark or otherwise, in this village!"

For the first time, Kamsa's face showed the first sign of emotion. His brows contracted, and he said in a louder tone, "I cannot leave here until my daughter has completed her education."

"You cannot stay!" squeaked the smaller man, appearing to have lost all control. He lunged at Kamsa, who leapt out of the way with surprising agility. Holding his hands up to fend off the attacker, Kamsa said, "I will not disturb you any more. I will have no more dialogues with you, and I will only work during the day. My only request to you is that you allow my daughter to attend school here."

"We have nothing against your daughter," consented the burly man. "She is welcome to attend school here, and meet our own children…but you, Kamsa…you must stay away."

Kamsa bowed his head in agreement, and turned. Shuffling slowly back to the door of his hut, he started to close it behind him.

"Wait!" The small man had recovered himself, and called out after Kamsa.

"Yes?" Kamsa turned to face the short-tempered aggressor, his visage once more covered in shadow.

"What is it you are always working on?"

A smile crept across Kamsa's face, and he shut the battered door carefully behind him, leaving the villagers standing on his doorstep as the sun rose majestically behind them.

THE FOLLOWING MORNING, as Kamsa sat in his workshop, he failed to notice a small girl slip into the room, and sit on a stool behind him. Although outside the window she leaned upon were others of her own age playing, she remained more interested in the man hunched over his workbench across the room.

After a few moments of silence, she asked him, "Father, what are you doing?"

"What?" Kamsa stopped his work, and turned. His

eyes widened at the sight of his daughter, and his lined face broke into a smile. Pulling a cloth out from under his workbench, he quickly covered up his work, and strode to the window. Dusting his hands off, he asked Rani, "You never play with the children. Why is that?"

Rani shrugged her shoulders, her wavy black hair moving up and down. "They don't do anything very interesting. They aren't *different* like you." She smiled eagerly up at her father as she said this. He laughed, and replied, "Different? What do you mean by that?"

Rani responded, "You can do things that the others can't. Even the other men in the village don't do the work you do. They do boring things, like chopping wood."

Kamsa chuckled, and ruffled Rani's hair. She turned to him, and, gathering up her courage, asked timidly, "What exactly do you do, Father? I wish you would show me."

Kamsa looked down at his daughter and smiled.

"I can…communicate with those who have passed on." His face glazed over as he said these words, and Kamsa removed his hand from Rani's head. She sat up straighter, hoping he would speak more, but Kamsa seemed oblivious to her sudden attentiveness. He gazed out the window at the other children, but his mind was once more upon his spellbook.

"But how, Father? How do you speak with them?" Rani's impatient voice seemed to bring Kamsa out of his reverie. He pointed out of the window, to the distant snow-capped peaks of the Himalayas.

"Do you see those mountains?"

Rani nodded vigorously, her eyes wide with excitement.

"At the top of the tallest peak in those mountains is a bamboo grove. I ventured there to meditate. After some time, my powers were granted."

Rani gave a sigh, and looked out at the mountains, wishing that she could see the grove. Then her small brows contracted, and she pulled at her father's shirt. He smiled down at her.

"What is it, my daughter?"

Rani's voice was no longer eager; it had been lowered to a frightened whisper, and Kamsa had to kneel down to listen.

"Mother isn't happy...she was saying she wants to leave. Doesn't she like me?"

Kamsa paused for a moment, while his daughter waited anxiously for his reply. He ran a hand through his unruly black hair as he spoke.

"Your mother isn't displeased with you. She is... Disappointed in me." As he said this, Kamsa threw a fleeting glance to his worktable, now covered in the large cloth.

"But why?" Rani looked shocked that anyone could be unhappy with her father. Kamsa looked amused for a moment, but then his face grew lined with worry once more as he thought of his wife.

"She has many reasons, my child. Many reasons...displeasing family is a terrible crime, one I suppose I have committed. I hope you will not do so."

"No, never!" The little girl's heart seemed to beat quickly if she even thought of disobeying her father. He smiled fondly at her, and stroked her dark hair.

"That is good." Kamsa's words were spoken without emotion, for his face had once more become a mask behind which his desire to complete the spellbook grew stronger with every moment. Rani looked at her father's strange expression, wishing more than ever that she would someday possess the talents Kamsa held, which would induct her into the strange world he lived in.

As the years passed and Rani grew older, Kamsa's affection for his precious book deepened. He spent increasingly long hours in his tiny, cramped workshop, and though he scarcely dared to admit it, he understood that the book was consuming him. The things he had put within it to allure men, common men who he believed to be inferior to him, were now beginning to grasp at his heart and tug at it.

As obsessed as he was with his brilliant creation, Kamsa was not blind to that which occurred around him. His wife, dissatisfied by both his neglect of his family and his refusal to find more than occasional odd jobs, planned to return to her own village. She insisted upon taking Rani with her, but failed.

"I won't go, Mother, I won't!" Rani sat stubbornly on the floor of the hut, her thin brown arms crossed defiantly. Her mother shouted sharply from outside the open door, "Come! Now! Your father will not take care of you."

"He will, he will, he loves me!" Rani shouted back angrily. Kamsa, sitting on his bench in the workshop, listened in silence.

"You are a foolish girl," spoke Rani's mother harshly. "You think that lazy man sitting hidden in his workshop can provide you with what you need? A husband, a house? No! He will do none of that, and you will end up a pauper as he is!" The door slammed with a bang, leaving Rani alone in the house, illuminated by a single window.

Kamsa sat in silence in his workshop for many moments, but did not go to comfort his daughter. Was his wife correct? Would he be unable to provide Rani with the things necessary in order to lead a good life? As he returned to work on the spellbook, Kamsa promised himself that no matter what happened, he would do anything to help his daughter.

A S HIS DAUGHTER GREW into a young woman, Kamsa began to fear the worst. He had no job, and therefore would be forced to sell his spellbook in order to give Rani a dowry for her marriage. Although he did not admit it to himself, Kamsa cared more for his spellbook than for his own daughter, despite the fact that she revered, even worshipped him. In order to convince his daughter to marry, Kamsa showed Rani the spellbook.

"I am going to show you what I have been working on for all these years." Kamsa sat at his workbench, facing Rani. His face was lined, and gray streaks ran through his hair. The young woman across from him sat listening intently, her dark eyes narrowed in concentration as he turned and lifted the spellbook into the air.

Suddenly the dim workshop was flooded with light. Rani, who had raised her hands to shield her eyes from the sudden brightness, slowly lowered them to gaze in awe at the book. It was thick, with rough, yellowing pages that had been unevenly cut. Dark brown leather with age spots and several rips that had been hastily mended with thin white thread covered the book. It was from behind this that a brilliant golden light seemed to pulsate, filling Rani with amazement and wonder.

"What is it, father?"

"The spellbook that I told you about so many years ago." Kamsa's voice was quiet and controlled, but he could not stop the triumph he felt from affecting his speech.

Rani watched the spellbook carefully. Her eyes narrowed slightly as she wondered whom else her father had shown the book to.

"Have you shown this to anyone else, father?"

Kamsa shook his head slowly. "No, I have not. It is a secret that I will trust no one but family with. Why do you ask this?"

Rani hesitated before replying timidly, "Haven't you ever worried that someone might steal it?"

This newly authoritative tone irked Kamsa, who returned the spellbook to the wooden workbench, and then covered it with a cloth. The moment the book left his hands, its glow faded, plunging the room into near darkness once more. Kamsa turned to Rani, his wrinkled hands folded in his lap.

"I have put the things that allure men within it. Power,

eternal life, and wealth—it is all possible for the one who possesses the spellbook."

Kamsa sighed, as though troubled by the words that he had just spoken. Rani frowned, trying to imagine why men would be lured by power and wealth. She was drawn from her reverie by her father's deep voice.

"There is something I need to speak with you about."

"Yes?" Rani's eyes widened slightly, as though fearing what her father would say next.

Kamsa took a deep breath to steady his body, which shook with the fear of parting with the beloved book. In a constricted voice, Kamsa said, "The time has come for you to be married. As I have no job to provide you with a proper dowry, you must accompany me to the next village, where we will proceed to sell the spellbook, and secure you a dowry."

"Why not this village?" Rani's voice sounded even smaller than when she had questioned her father earlier.

Kamsa replied, "The men here will not buy the spellbook. They see me as a crazy fool." Rani quickly lowered her eyes at this comment, but did not contest it.

He continued, "Once we find a buyer for the spellbook, I will find an appropriate suitor for you. With the dowry the book will bring us, we will not have trouble finding you one."

This small speech seemed to have taken what little energy Kamsa possessed. He sank back against the workbench, and closed his eyes. Creating the spellbook had made him a man far older than his years, Kamsa thought to himself. Soon, he would be free to rest and enjoy his life, free of all responsibility and burdens. To his surprise, Kamsa did not feel the guilt he had expected for not caring for his daughter as he had when she was young. Those memories seemed as though they had belonged to a different man; Kamsa regarded them as mere dreams or figments of his imagination, nothing more.

"Father?"

"Yes?" His voice was rasping, and he found that his eyes were barely able to make out the silhouette of Rani, even in the faint moonlight pouring through the window.

"I don't want to be married."

Kamsa could not believe his ears. He listened intently, but no more words were spoken; the only noise was the chirping of crickets in the still night. He asked quietly, "What do you mean?"

"I wish to go meditate in the bamboo grove, as you have done. If I can achieve what you have done, I will be content with my life. You should not have to sell the spellbook; it means too much to you."

Shock flooded Kamsa's body, rendering him speechless for several moments. What was his daughter saying? The words of his irate wife echoed in his ears: *You think that lazy man sitting hidden in his workshop can provide you with what you need? A husband, a house? No! He will do none of that, and you will end up a pauper as he is!*

Kamsa doubted himself for a moment. Had he not provided his daughter with that? Had he not offered to throw away his life's work in order to help her? He felt anger rising within him, first a faint coil of smoke, then a blazing fire.

"You must get married to a man chosen by your family; if you do not, our society will shun you forever. There is no question." He fought to control his tongue, to stop himself from lashing out at his daughter.

"I will not marry a man you choose for me. I wish to achieve something in my life!" Her words goaded Kamsa to his feet.

"Your job in life is not to achieve things! I have proposed selling my life's work to secure you an appropriate future, and in return you reject my offer!" Kamsa's voice rose angrily.

Rani did not cower before his anger, but stood up and said in a tearful voice, "All I want is to be like you! Please, Father, give me the opportunity!"

Kamsa raised his arm as though to strike Rani; she crumpled to the ground, her hands held above her head in a weak defense. He grabbed her by the arm and shouted, "I will lock you in your room until the day you are married if necessary!" Gripping Rani's arm tightly, Kamsa dragged her across the dimly lit workshop, ignoring her stifled sobs.

Crossing the dingy hallway of their home, Kamsa pulled Rani up roughly. She cried, "Father, no!" She struggled for several moments before freeing herself from Kamsa's grip. Staggering, Rani said with wide eyes that were rapidly filling with tears, "I have told you already I will not marry.

You cannot force me to do so!" Her voice reached a hysterical pitch as she spoke the last words, enraging Kamsa further. Seizing her more firmly by the upper arm, he ignored her squeak of pain and pulled her along.

Throwing open a wooden door that led into another room with a tiny window, he pushed Rani into it. Looking around the bare room in fury, Kamsa clenched his hand tightly around the rotting wood of the old door. Ignoring the hinges' creaks and groans of protest, Kamsa slammed the door shut in his anger. Blood pounded through his head.

"You will get married, if it is the last thing I do! I did not suffer this life so that you could turn on me and defy me!" Kamsa roared angrily through the door, his voice echoing up and down the darkened hallway.

Pounding at the door, Rani shouted, "Father, please, let me out! Father!" Her cries seemed to be swallowed by the silence that filled the house. Sinking to the floor, Rani leaned against the old wooden door, the hiccupping sobs filling her body with grief.

Seconds, minutes and hours ticked by, and still Rani sat silently by the door, her dark eyes red-rimmed from crying. There were no signs of life in the house; she feared her father would not return to free her. In these moments of fear, Rani would shake the door furiously and pound it with her hands, reducing herself to tears once more. She would then sink down slowly, and curl up into as small a ball as her body would allow, as though she wished she could disappear from this world entirely.

As the sun rose after her long night of imprisonment,

Rani stood, and walked over to the window. From it, she could see the Himalayas, their snowcapped peaks shining majestically in the early morning light. Her sorrows and worries forgotten for the moment, Rani closed her eyes, and imagined the grove that she had yearned to see since she was a little girl. The bamboo seemed to rustle in her ears and the peaceful sense of pride and achievement she had always imagined engulfed her.

The sound of a woman's voice calling to her children forced Rani to open her eyes. She looked away from the mountains and down at her hands, which lay clasped upon the muddy windowsill. A thought came to Rani's mind, one so daring that she quickly forced it out. But it soon found its way back in and slowly began to entwine itself in her mind.

Rani's heart thudded fiercely inside her chest when she thought of running away from home. No one in her village had ever dreamed of doing such a thing, she told herself. It was the first time she had thought of committing such an act, but as Rani looked at her bleak surroundings, she knew that she could not allow her father to follow society's laws to arrange a marriage for her. The very idea repulsed Rani.

Feeling the pace of her heart quicken again, Rani wondered if she was strong enough to flee from her father in order to achieve what she truly wanted. As she hesitated, she thought of how her father had controlled her during her childhood, and how she had blindly obeyed him without question...but how could she have known that the man she revered was bound by the shackles of society, and would therefore never let her out of the cage she had been so cruelly locked in?

Rani felt a new emotion surge through her legs, propelling her onto the windowsill itself: anger at her father for deceiving her with his lies of his superiority to other men.

She had only respected him because she had believed that her father's magic made him impervious to the worries that other villagers seemed to struggle with. Rani wondered if her father's magic had ever truly freed him from the dark life he was now living. Rani felt her spine prickle as she thought once more of attaining her father's abilities, but the prickle was one of fear, not excitement. Rani ignored this sudden fear of magic—she knew that she would not succumb to it the way her father had.

From her perch on the windowsill, the Himalayas seemed even closer. Rani looked back one more time at the room, biting her lip, but then her father's words rang through her brain: *"I did not suffer this life so that you could turn on me and defy me!"*

Kamsa's words cut through Rani's heart like a knife. She felt angrier than ever that her father, a man consumed by his own magic, had dared tell her that she could not do all that he had done and more. The desire to escape grew so strong that Rani could no longer resist it.

Without looking back, Rani climbed out of her prison, and began to run towards the distant mountain peaks, her heart beating like a drum within her chest.

As THE DAY WORE ON, however, Rani felt as though her journey would never end. She had not thought to bring food or water with her, and was dreadfully thirsty. Her feet lagged, and as the sun slowly set behind her, Rani felt for the first time that she was only an unimportant speck in the world around her, unnoticed and unneeded.

Sitting down to rest, Rani felt she could no longer go on. She thought of what her father would do if she returned from her excursion. The thought of being locked in the windowless room again seemed horrible. This terrifying image brought her weary body to a standing position once more, and she continued walking.

As THE SUN SLOWLY bade goodbye to the golden cornfields and began to sink behind the horizon in the distance, Rani finally reached the foothills of one of the many mountain peaks that stretched farther than her eye could see. Between Rani and the steep slope of the mountain lay only a cornfield, the golden stalks waving gently in the wind.

Emboldened by the sight of her goal, Rani strode faster through the weeds. In her haste she failed to notice a leopard crouching hidden among the stalks, its golden coat blending almost perfectly. The leopard waited for its prey to draw nearer, and then pounced on the unsuspecting Rani from behind. Her loud scream echoed ominously across the lands she had traversed alone.

The leopard ripped her thick ribbon out of her hair with its menacing claw, and her long braid came loose.

With immense effort, Rani pushed the leopard away from her, rolled away from its vicious claws, and ran across the field, her hair flying out behind her. With a ferocious roar, the leopard leapt upon Rani, knocking her to the ground. The leopard raised its massive paw, preparing to strike. She trembled beneath the beast, and raised her hand to shield her face.

In the distance, Li Shen, a Chinese general, sat astride his white horse, whose coat glowed by the light of the moon. His eyes widened at the sight of the woman and the leopard, and he murmured to the horse, which then began to canter through the cornfields, its tail streaming behind it, as fine as silk. The man drew a long sword as the horse started to gallop. He cried out, urging it on with nearly unintelligible words.

As the horse galloped past the leopard, Li Shen shouted. The beast turned its head, and was struck by the sword, across the face. It drew back with a howl, blood spattering the golden stalks. Rani rolled away from the leopard, and sat, frozen, amid the corn.

The horse had slowed now, and turned to face the leopard, the man holding his sword majestically. The leopard eyed him malevolently, blood darkening its spotted golden coat. Li Shen clicked his tongue, and his horse moved a few steps forward reluctantly. He brandished his sword. At the sight of the instrument that had drawn its blood, the leopard shrank further and further into the cornfield, until it could no longer be seen. The man waited for several moments until he was sure it was gone.

Then, dismounting from his horse, Li Shen offered his hand to Rani. She took it without hesitation, although she was frightened. Her father had always forbidden her to speak with foreign men whenever they had come to the village. Rani hoped to escape the man as soon as possible, and continue her journey alone.

Helping her up, Li Shen asked, "Why are you here? Young women seldom travel to the mountains alone."

Rani hesitated, but then replied, "I am searching for a bamboo grove."

Li Shen nodded gravely, and asked, "The sacred bamboo grove? I thought it was only a myth."

"No, it is not. My father meditated there, and I wish to do the same."

Li Shen looked around, as though expecting to see an old man. "Where is your father?"

"I have run away from home," said Rani defiantly.

After her statement a long silence followed, during which Rani stood staring at the strange man in front of her as though daring him to send her back to her prison. She felt her heart thudding against her chest as she watched him contemplate her for a moment, one of his hands rubbing his chin thoughtfully, while the other held his horse's bridle.

Li Shen was surprised by the defiance of the young woman. She had shown bravery that he had not seen from many people—including some of his own peers. Her dark eyes gazed intensely into his own, while he thought of how he could help her to achieve her goal.

"Let me escort you through the mountains. It would be a pity if you were caught in the claws of a leopard once more."

"I don't need help." Her haughty tone caused Li Shen to raise his eyebrows. She turned away from him, and began to walk briskly through the cornfield, pushing aside the tall stalks as she went. Li Shen jogged after her, his horse in tow.

"Everyone needs help at one point in their life."

Rani did not stop walking, but simply replied, "Then I plan to only have help when I am to be buried after my death."

"Why are you so reluctant to accept my offer?" Li Shen asked, puzzled by her rebuffs.

The woman finally paused, and turned to look at him. Li Shen saw a flicker of fear in her eyes, and his brows furrowed in confusion. Surely this lady, with the spirit of a warrior, could not be afraid of something?

"What is it that frightens you?" He spoke gently. She looked away from him, as though unable to see him while she spoke of her weaknesses.

"My father has forbidden me to take the company of men who are not of my race."

Li Shen nodded in an understanding manner. Rani quickly looked up at him, then away again. A silence fell between them once more as they stood still among the corn. Li Shen quietly asked, "Will you continue to obey your father now that you have left your home and your life behind?"

It was Rani's turn to frown now; her lips pressed into a thin line before she spoke, forcing the words out as though she could not believe they were true.

"No. I will not have to obey him."

Li Shen smiled, and bowed low to her, his right knee pressing against the rough soil of the field. Offering his hand to her for the second time that night, Li Shen asked, "Then will you allow me to escort you through the mountains, so that no further danger or catastrophe shall befall you?"

Rani agreed. Li Shen helped her onto his horse, and led it through the cornfield towards the mountains.

As they traveled through the mountains, Rani and Li Shen became accustomed to one another. Rani liked Li Shen for his gentle, kind nature, and he enjoyed learning what Rani knew about the Himalayas and magic, knowledge which her father had occasionally imparted to her when she was younger.

In the year that they wove through the mountains toward the bamboo grove, Rani and Li Shen slowly began to fall in love. Although Rani was blissfully happy with Li Shen, she felt a stab deep within her heart when she thought of her father, and what he would say if he saw her with a man who was not Indian. As time passed, however, Rani's feelings of foreboding began to fade, until they had almost vanished.

Rani and Li Shen feared the discovery of their romance, and were unsure of whether to return to their respective homes or continue their lives together. They soon realized, however, that they could not live without each other. Rani and Li Shen chose to live in the mountains forever, because they knew that their families would not approve of their love—their families would not be happy that their races had mixed.

After one year in hiding in the bamboo grove, Rani bore Li Shen's child. The couple named their beautiful daughter Tien Ming, so that she might have the power of the sacred Tien Shan Mountains, and the elegance of the great Ming dynasty. They knew that her birth in the bamboo grove would grant her the powers attributed to her name.

Despite the fact that she had a new family, Rani often thought of her father, the family she had left behind. Pangs of guilt and fear began to creep over her again, for she knew that her father might find her and punish her for what she had done. Rani, because of her child, was now an outcast in her own village.

IN THE MEANTIME, as Rani had predicted, Kamsa had been searching for her far and wide. After Rani's disappearance, Kamsa had felt as though the sun had gone from the world. He was never happy, even when working on spellbook. Kamsa often found himself turning to speak to the little girl on the stool in his workshop, only to find the seat empty, and his house unoccupied by his family.

Unable to bear life without his daughter, Kamsa meditated to Lord Ganesha to remove all obstacles from his path. Lord Ganesha obliged, and Kamsa found that his fears and worries of what had become of his daughter melted away, leaving him only to dwell on finding his beloved child. His mind cleared, Kamsa was granted a vision by the gods.

He saw a beautiful clearing. It stood atop the mountains. Bamboo trees towered over a meditation rock at the grove's center, shielding it from outside view. He recognized it as the sacred grove where he had been granted his magical powers through meditation. Under the cover of the trees was a primitive hut, made out of bamboo. Within the hut, Kamsa saw his daughter, glowing with happiness and pride. Next to her stood a man of Chinese origin, his dark eyes fixated upon Rani adoringly. She held a small bundle of blankets in her arms tenderly, from among which Kamsa could see a small tuft of black hair, and a tiny hand waving in the air.

In an instant, it was clear to Kamsa—his daughter had conceived a child with a man who was not of their race, instantly making her an outcast among her own people, a fate Kamsa had never wanted for Rani. With worry and anger clouding both his mind and judgment, Kamsa vowed to separate his daughter and the infidel who had fathered the baby girl in the hope that Rani would forget the mistake she had made, and repent. Kamsa took the long, familiar path to the grove where he had meditated many years ago.

THROWING OPEN THE door to the hut, Kamsa grabbed Rani by the hair. Dragging her outside to the central clearing, he threw her to the ground.

"What have you done?" Kamsa's voice was harsh with anger.

"Father, please, try and understand. I——" Rani's voice was filled with fear and sadness; the prick of guilt that had once filled her heart had now returned.

"You have betrayed your people, your race by having a child with this man!" From within his pocket, Kamsa drew a blade, and held it against Rani's neck. She screamed, tears running down her face. To her surprise, Rani found that however much her father berated her, she did not regret the birth of her child.

"Father, no! Please, give me another chance to redeem myself!"

Kamsa raised his blade without hesitation, preparing to kill his daughter. As he brought it down, Li Shen rushed forward, and pushed the angry man's blade away.

Kamsa's eyes flashed.

"You fool! Keep out of these family matters, or I will kill you as well!"

"Please, do not kill your daughter, sir. I beg of you, do anything but that." Li Shen clasped his hands together in a sign of respect to Kamsa as he spoke. The three remained silent for many moments, until the baby began to wail from the hut.

Kamsa's lips tightened.

"Show me the girl."

Rani hurried to the hut, and soon returned with the baby. Kamsa looked down at the child. It would be very beautiful; there was no doubt about it. The brown skin and almond-shaped eyes resembled Rani's own.

"She looks like us, Father."

"Looks cannot hide her mixed blood." Kamsa's words were filled with venom. Rani's eyes filled with tears of anguish, and she looked away from her father, still cradling the baby.

"Take the baby away," said Kamsa to Li Shen. "We do not want her mixed blood to blacken our name. If you ever return here, or come near my daughter, I will kill you. Do you understand?"

"Yes, sir." Li Shen took the baby girl from Rani, but the two did not dare hug in front of Kamsa. Li Shen opened his mouth as though he wished to speak, but the murderous look upon Kamsa's face silenced his tongue. Without looking back, Li Shen climbed over the protective rock wall around the grove, and vanished.

"Whether she has mixed blood or not, that child is your granddaughter," Rani said quietly.

Kamsa replied coldly, "She is no relation of mine."

Rani felt a cold sinking within her stomach as her father's words pierced her heart. Kamsa spoke again, in the same cold voice.

"You can no longer return to the village. You have dishonored me, Rani. I can no longer call you my daughter."

"If I am no longer your daughter, then why did you take me from my family?" Rani's words echoed around the empty clearing; Kamsa had exited, leaving her alone.

In the weeks that followed, Rani rid herself of all

things that connected her to her past life, such as the jewelry her father had given her. She instead turned her focus to meditating in order to achieve the magical powers she had so longed for. Unfortunately, it was not to be so. Rani's dreams had now changed, and all she could think of was her missing child and Li Shen. Her mind would not allow her to go to the realms beyond the world of men to reach the spirits, because she was tethered to the world of humans by her love for Li Shen and her child, Tien.

Rani was never seen again. In fact, it seemed as though after the loss of her family, she had simply vanished. Similarly, Kamsa never returned to his village after condemning Rani to the life of a hermit.

O N HIS WAY DOWN from the mountains, Li Shen was caught in a snowstorm. The wind whipped wildly around his face, and even as he raised his arms to protect himself and his daughter from the strange, biting wind, Li Shen knew a dangerous magical force had caught him. Instead of trying to fight, Li Shen fell to his knees, unable to see in front of him because of the snow that flew through the air. Cold flakes hit his face, and ran down his reddened cheeks like icy tears. Scooting along the ground, Li Shen ran his hands along the land in front of him, searching for something. Finally, his nearly numb fingers felt rough, wind-beaten leaves and several sturdy branches. Leaning close to the branches, he carefully moved the bundle of blankets that contained his daughter carefully between the branches. When he was sure she was secure,

Li Shen stood up, and raised his arms in defeat. The snowstorm howled, and swept Li Shen away. As quickly as it had begun, the storm and the wind vanished, leaving flurries of snow flying through the air.

Many hours later, an old woman shuffled through the snow. She frowned, the wrinkles upon her face thrown into sharp relief by the fading rays of the sun. The tracks left by the strange wind that had taken Li Shen away puzzled the woman. She bent down, and ran her finger through the snow, as if trying to feel the presence of what had been there before her.

A tiny sneeze from the nearest bush startled the old woman. She straightened up, her long gray braid swinging as she did so. Her intense, deep brown eyes scanned the white landscape around her.

"Hello? Who is there?"

A wail answered her voice. The woman fell to her knees at once, and began to dig away the snow that had since weighed down the branches of the bush that Li Shen had placed his daughter in. When at last the baby's face came into view, the Chinese woman pulled the child out of the snow. Lifting the young girl into the air, the old woman smiled.

"How did you survive that storm? Who are your parents?"

The baby gurgled joyfully in response. The woman laughed and said, "Look at me, child, and show me what you have seen in your short lifetime." Her eyes gazed thoughtfully into the baby's smaller ones. The woman's eyes widened.

"So you are Li Shen's daughter, Tien Ming…You are not from here. Those eyes, that skin…" The woman's voice trailed off, and she looked at the child, tears filling her eyes. Drawing the child close to her, she said, "My name is Wise Woman. I will help you, Tien, because you have been wronged already in your life…and because a difficult and dangerous path lies ahead of you."

The baby pointed to a small group of huts at the base of the mountains, to which a winding path led the way.

"Yes, that is my home…and yours too now, I suppose." Wise Woman chuckled as she began to walk back down the mountain path, the dying rays of the sun behind her.

Chapter One

An Untimely Passing

My heart beat quickly as I peered through the gaps in the tree's large branches. There was no one on the dusty road as far as I could see. I shifted my position ever so slightly, and shielded my eyes from the bright sun that filtered through the leaves. Pushing aside the rough brown branches tentatively, I looked down onto the road once more. It remained empty.

Sinking back against the large branch that had been my most recent hideaway, I sighed. *Maybe they won't find me today,* I thought to myself.

Suddenly, a cry sounded from down the road. I jolted, and scrambled higher into the tree, my skinny brown legs trembling with fear.

"There she is!" A boy skidded to a stop under the tree, dust rising around his dirty, ragged clothes.

Other children were surrounding the first boy now; my heart was thudding in my chest.

"Climb the tree! That'll scare her down!" The children were encouraging the boy now. He grinned wickedly, and called up to me, "How's the view, Darkie? We almost missed you in the shadows!"

The other children laughed cruelly, and I frantically brushed away the tears that came all too easily. I clung helplessly to the branch of the tree, watching as the boy began to climb the trunk. The others laughed and jeered from the ground.

"Come on Darkie!" The boy was mere inches away now. "We won't hurt you...much."

"Get away from me!" I yelled, backing away on the tree branch. The boy followed me until we were both out on the branch. It swayed dangerously under the weight of his larger, heavier body. My tormentor's pale skin and slanted eyes glowed in the bright sunlight, contrasting with my own darker skin and rounder eyes.

"Come on, Darkie!" He reached into his pocket and brought out a round, flat stone. I eyed it apprehensively. The boy chuckled.

"What's the matter?"

"Call me Tien. I don't like the name Darkie." I spoke authoritatively, my voice firm when I addressed the bully.

"Your name doesn't fit you!" the boy said loudly. The crowd of my peers below shouted and laughed in agreement. I backed away even further on the branch, which began to crack under the weight of two people.

"I'm no different from you!" I cried the words desperately and without conviction.

The boy clutched the stone tighter in his hand, and advanced towards me on the tree branch.

"You don't even look like us," he said with a short laugh. "How can you be the same?"

The simple words cut through my heart like a knife. Staggering backwards, I finally heard the tree branch snap, but the shouts of the boy and others below me were only secondary to the mind-numbing pain of isolation that once again plagued me.

As we hit the ground, I scrambled to my feet, miraculously unhurt from the long fall. One look to my left however, and I saw that the boy had not fared as well. He lay facedown and did not stir.

The children rushed towards him, but their lack of concern for me was a relief; I quickly backed away, hoping to escape.

The boy sat up groggily as his companions revived him, looking around. His eyes lit upon me, and I turned to run, but it was too late.

"Get her!" he shouted, his words slurred from pain. The other children turned, pulling rocks from within their rags.

The first one hit my arm, followed by a stinging, red

welt. I sprinted away from the tree and down the dusty road, my bare feet kicking up dirt behind me. I could hear the heavy breathing of the children as they followed me down the path, which only caused me to run faster.

We entered the center of the village, which was marked by the cluster of open-air stalls selling a variety of foods. Buyers haggled with the old, toothless men who owned the shops, creating a lively atmosphere. The early morning sun beat down upon me as I wove my way through the crowd of shoppers, hoping to hide from my cruel peers.

It was not to be so. As I finally emerged back onto the narrow, tree-lined path, a glance over my shoulder told me that the others were still in pursuit. My lungs were beginning to burn, but I forced myself to continue at a slow jog.

The second rock hit me squarely in the back. I doubled over with shooting pains up and down my spine. Through narrowed eyelids, I saw the children circle me, their hands devoid of rocks, balled into fists.

"What happened with the branch, Darkie? Why weren't you hurt?" The jeering tone shook me.

"I didn't do anything! I just fell from the branch."

"But you weren't hurt!" the children exclaimed. They murmured among themselves. I turned slowly on the spot, scrutinizing the angry young faces that were so dissimilar to my own. The shade from the trees created only the faintest patches upon their otherwise pale, flawless skin, while my own skin appeared nearly black.

But why hadn't I been hurt? The thought had barely formed in my mind when the boy nearest me ran forward, his fists up, and delivered a direct punch to my stomach. I doubled over, and swung out with my own arm, but missed. The other children were drawing closer to me now, and I knew inwardly that I would not be able to win the battle— this, however, did not stop me from raising my own hands in defense.

"You won't be able to fight us," said one of the children to me. "There are so many of us, but only one of you!"

In response, I raised my fists higher.

"Get out of my way!" I barreled through the circle of children, but they threw me back forcefully. I landed hard against the ground, feeling blood run down my cheek. Sitting up, I wiped the blood away, feeling it sting with the dirt from my fingers. The children closed in once more, laughing as I struggled to stand.

"What is going on here?" The elderly voice lifted my heart. I raised my head, a smile upon my face.

A Chinese woman stood a few feet down the path, an orange in one hand and a cane in her other. Although she was old, and her skin wrinkled, the woman's hair still contained traces of its youthful black, visible in the pieces that fell from her bun. She leaned against her sturdy cane as she questioned the children a second time.

"What has happened here? Why do you all gather so?"

The children seemed afraid to respond. They shifted uncomfortably back and forth, their hands now behind their backs and the once sinister faces docile. I dared not stand up for fear that they would later punish me for re-vealing the source of my injury to Wise Woman.

"Nothing has happened, Wise Woman," said one girl. "We were only playing."

The intense, dark eyes of Wise Woman surveyed the children. She did not appear convinced by their innocence, and did not pretend to be so. Without hesitation, she hob-bled forward with her cane, and shooed the children aside. They scattered unwillingly to reveal me, cowering with my dirty hand against my face to hide the injury.

Wise Woman held out a hand to me, leaning on her cane, and I took it. She helped me up, and said quietly, "Remove your hand from your face."

I shook my head violently, and my hand trembled in fear within her own. She squeezed my hand gently and said, "Tien, do not be afraid. Remove your hand."

I took a deep breath, and looked into Wise Woman's eyes. She nodded encouragingly at me, and I removed my hand from my bloody cheek. Wise Woman looked at the scrape, which had since stopped bleeding. Lifting my left arm, she examined the welt upon it. I watched her face while she did this, noting that the patches of shade on her skin were not as dark as mine. Despite Wise Woman's acts of kindness, I felt isolated once more by my unique appearance.

Taking my hand in her own, Wise Woman murmured, "We should go home now."

To the children at large, she said calmly, "You should not be so far on the outskirts of town. Return to the marketplace."

"Yes, Wise Woman," all the children murmured. I watched them scuttle away down the dusty path until they turned the corner, vanishing from sight. Wise Woman patted me on the back gently, and said, "We should go home. I will be able to clean your cheek off then."

I nodded, and we walked in silence for several moments before Wise Woman asked, "So where did you hide today?"

"The big tree," I muttered. "On the other edge of the village."

She nodded. "But they still found you...Maybe you should stay in the house tomorrow."

"They would just come in after you left. It happened last time."

Wise Woman nodded again, her head moving slowly. We were nearing the end of the dusty path now, and I could see the familiar thatched hut, standing solitary with the picturesque mountains behind it.

"I cannot stop them, Tien. The villagers refuse to believe that their children give you these injuries."

"Then where do they think these bruises come from?" I asked indignantly, holding up my arm. Wise Woman studied the dark bruises of varying size and color before responding.

"They think that you are...different. That you might be the cause of your own bruises."

My heart sank.

"Am I?" I asked Wise Woman.

"Are you what?" She appeared confused by my question.

"Am I different?"

"Only in the way that you are kinder than the others of your age, and more compassionate than many of the adults in the village," replied Wise Woman. I nodded, but remained unconvinced.

We had reached the hut. I opened the door for my guardian, and she smiled in thanks. Handing me her orange, Wise Woman asked, "Do you want something to eat? I can make something."

I shook my head, and shut the door of the hut behind me. Proceeding to the small wooden table in the center of the hut, I sat down. Wise Woman busied herself at the clay oven at the other end of the room, heating water.

"Watch the water, Tien," she said to me. "I have to get a rag for your cheek."

Hobbling into a small adjacent room, Wise Woman left me alone to stare out the window of the hut at the beautiful mountains. After a few moments, I heard the steady thud of her cane once more as she slowly made her way towards the table.

"You like the mountains, don't you?" She chuckled as I nodded emphatically.

"I wish I could live in the mountains," I told Wise Woman. She smiled at me.

"And maybe you will someday. Now, would you like to hear a story?"

She sat down next to me at the table, holding a wet rag

in one hand and a bucket of warm water in the other. Dabbing at my cheek, Wise Woman began.

"There once was a young man. He lived in a small village, and although he was bright, this man was looked down upon because he was poor. One day, the man decided to travel high into the Himalayas, because he had heard that a magical grove existed there."

As Wise Woman cleaned my cheek, her free hand moved in complicated motions, conjuring up beams of light from her fingers that reflected on the wall. The rough outline of mountain peaks appeared on the brown bamboo reeds, vanishing as the shape of a human replaced it. I listened intently, curious as to what would happen next.

"The man found the grove, after many months of searching. It was upon the highest peak of the tallest mountain, and was protected by a bamboo forest that grew within it and a rock wall that surrounded it. The man lived in the bamboo grove, and meditated to the gods in the hope that he would be blessed with magical powers."

"Why did he want to have magical powers?"

"He wished to make a spellbook that would contain the secret to immortality. Once he conveyed this wish to the gods, the man was granted his powers—his dream however, would take time to achieve. He returned to his village at the base of the Himalaya Mountains, and married a woman. She gave birth to a beautiful baby girl."

The shapes twisted, and I could see two figures cradling a small child, their shapes strangely stretched and manipulated by the bamboo wall.

"What happened next?" I asked eagerly.

"Alas, the man and his family soon became very poor, because he would not work—the spellbook became his only passion. They soon lost all their money, and the wife grew discontent with her husband. The pair often fought, but even her threats to leave the household would not stop the man from creating spell after spell to put within the magical book. Eternal wealth and beauty, spells to obtain skills normally unavailable to man, such as flight and control of the seas—he desperately tried to explain the value of these to his wife, but she would not listen. Finally, one day, the wife left the village, and was never seen again."

One of the figures vanished from the wall, and another sunk down, and shook with what I knew to be sobs. I gasped.

"What happened? Was the man sad?"

Wise Woman turned to look at me, her brown eyes full of sorrow.

"The man was upset that his wife had left, but he could not stop work on his spellbook. Within the book, he continued to put enchantments and spells that would surely be coveted by the kings and queens of every land. But the spell that the man was most proud of was one that he had created himself: the secret to immortality."

My eyes widened.

"You mean the holder of the spellbook could live forever?"

Wise Woman nodded. "Yes. The man sealed the spellbook, placing a spell that would not allow it to be opened until the one who possessed the password would be able to reopen the spellbook, and use the magic within it."

She dropped her hands. The images vanished, and the beams returned to her fingers, leaving the walls bare and dark.

"What happened to the spellbook?" I asked.

Wise Woman shrugged.

"It is difficult to say...no one knows where it is, or even what the password is. Now go outside and play!" Wise Woman chased me out of the hut playfully, but it was difficult for me to stop thinking about what I had just heard.

This soon became my favorite story, out of all the ones Wise Woman would tell me about. Dragons, tigers, and princesses from faraway lands did not interest me as they did others; instead, I enjoyed listening to the strange tale of the man and his beloved spellbook. I felt a strange connection to the story, and could almost feel the emotions of the people within it as though they were my own. If Wise Woman saw anything strange about my obsession with the tale, she said nothing.

Unfortunately, stories did not ease the pain of the teasing and jeering I received from other children in the village. Because of my lonely existence, I often resorted to eavesdropping on the elders of the village for entertainment. These discussions were normally of little interest to me, until I once heard my own name spoken of.

It was a warm, breezy day. I had been playing alone, outside my hut, when Wise Woman came out, her gray robes wrapped around her even in the bright sunlight.

"Where are you going?"

"I must meet with the elders, little one. Stay here. I will be back soon."

I stood and watched sadly as Wise Woman walked down the path, and turned left, towards the elder's meeting place, a hut on the other end of the village. I waited a few moments until I was sure Wise Woman had gone. Then, with excitement rushing through my veins, I hurried after her.

Skirting the children in the center of the village and slipping between the women arguing in the market, I saw Wise Woman entering the elder's hut. Crouching down, I crawled towards the window in the hut, under which there were tall bamboo plants, in a group large enough to hide me. I leapt into the bamboo stalks, and was able to hear clearly every word that was spoken by the elders.

"Wise Woman, time is up. You must tell her." I did not recognize the voice, but my interest was piqued. Who did Wise Woman have to tell what?

"Tien is too young to know of the spellbook." Wise Woman's voice was defiant. I felt my heart leap in a mixture of excitement and fear.

"But you yourself told us only a few weeks ago that you have already told it to her in the form a folktale. She must take responsibility as a part of the family that created the spellbook. It is her duty to find it, and now she must do so. If the Force catches her, it will take the password from Tien, and open the book."

So the folktale had been about my family! I found my-self suddenly unable to breathe, as though invisible hands had constricted my windpipe. The longer I considered this impossible possibility, the more it seemed to make sense to me. Why else would I have felt a special connection to the story, and the emotions of the people within it?

Suddenly, Wise Woman's voice rang out loudly from within the hut, jolting me out of my thoughts.

"She cannot know yet! Placing a burden so large on one so young is a terrible thing to do. I will not tell Tien anything until the Force comes searching for her."

I frowned to myself. What was this Force that would take the spellbook from me? I felt a shiver run down my spine as I thought of the Force. Pushing it to the back of my mind, I continued to listen intently.

There was a dull clunk as a staff banged against the floor.

"That time will be all too soon, Wise Woman! Please, consider someone other than Tien or yourself for a mo-ment. The entire village will be destroyed if the Force comes here."

"You are the one who refuses to think of Tien. She would be devastated if she knew her parents were still alive, and that the Force had taken them. I do not wish to harm a child who is already singled out and wounded by her own peers."

"But if she knew that she alone held the password to the spellbook, and that in finding the book she would find her parents...that would mean a life with people of her own race!" The voices sounded eager, and I couldn't help but feel as though they were right. I longed more than anything to find people of my own kind, and to be accepted. At that moment, I made up my mind that I would bring my parents back to life, no matter what it took. I envisioned myself trekking through the mountains, Wise Woman by my side. We soon found my parents, and were able to live together in another village, far away from the mean-spirited children of my current home.

Wise Woman's angry voice cut through my daydreaming for a second time.

"If you hope that Tien will return here with the spellbook to give you all the secret of immortality, you are wrong. The secrets within the spellbook will not be revealed to anyone." Wise Woman spoke stiffly.

I felt my heart perform another leap, and I clutched my chest, fearful that my heart would jump right out of me. How could I control the spellbook? If I did manage to open the spellbook, or even to find it, would I grant the elders the secrets of eternal wealth, beauty and immortality?

More to avoid answering the difficult questions in my head than anything else, I quelled the inner voices, and listened as another Elder said disgustedly, "You misjudge us, Wise Woman."

"And you misjudge children. I—" Wise Woman stopped mid-sentence, only a moment after I shifted slightly within the bamboo. I froze with fear, and heard the scraping of a chair as she stood up. The door to my left was flung open, and through the green bamboo leaves, I saw the bottom of Wise Woman's gray robe.

Before I knew what was happening, she had dragged me out of the bamboo by my ear, and flung me to the ground. Dust from the ground rose around me, and I coughed.

"What did you hear?" Her voice was angry and demanding; I opened my mouth, and gaped wordlessly, unable to form words of any kind. From the corner of my eye I saw the other elders watching me, a mixture of fear and surprise upon their faces.

"N-nothing, I swear!"

"Never listen again, do you understand me? Forget what you have heard here."

Wise Woman's voice had lost all anger, and was replaced by fear. I did not understand what I had done wrong, but ran away from the hut, looking back to see the strange look upon my guardian's face.

This, of course, only increased my curiosity about the spellbook. The thought that the key to my past and perhaps a happier future lay within my reach drove me mad; I would find myself hoping for it to be true, but at the same time telling myself that it was impossible to wish for a life other than the one I already led.

This silent battle raged within my head for the next few years. I was too frightened to ever bring up the subject with Wise Woman again, and she followed my example, acting as though that terrible day had never existed.

O NE DARK NIGHT, I awoke to a cry from Wise
Woman. Upon entering her room, I found her doubled over in pain by the window, her eyes wide with fear.
When she saw me, she made frantic motions with her
hands. I came forward, worried.

"Are you all right? Let me fetch the doctor." I attempted to keep panic out of my voice; Wise Woman looked
very ill, and I feared that she would not survive the night.
Shaking her head, Wise Woman whispered, "No doctor
can help me now." After those words, speech seemed to
fail her. She hobbled to her bed, and from under her pil-
low removed a package and a folded piece of paper. Placing
them inside a dark brown woolen sack, she handed it to
me. My hands grasped hers, and I felt a chill creep down
my spine; her hands felt like ice.

Shudders ran through Wise Woman's body, and she
lay upon the bed, her eyes still wide, as though she feared
she would fall asleep. I placed my hand in hers, and sat
by her bedside for many long moments. She gripped my
hand tightly as the spasms continued to shake her body.
I held onto her firmly, and unfolded the letter with my
free hand.

Dear Tien,

*There were not many times in your childhood when I was
truly angry with you. The only time I felt anger lick my insides
like an angry flame was when you were very young, and you heard
the elders speak of an ancient spellbook, one that held the secret
to immortality.*

I will not go into more detail here; it is clear to both of us that you have not forgotten the events of that day, but have possibly only wondered why I did not tell you.

The truth is, the fact that I hid such an important part of your past and future from you displeased many of the elders; they hoped that you would find the spellbook and give them immortality, beauty, wealth, and power beyond their dreams. I fought the terrible human emotion of greed throughout your childhood years, but I realized that I would not be able to stop the elders forever; it was like a rushing river that threatened to drown me.

Those times are now past; you must forget the elders and their sinister qualities, as your true quest is far more challenging.

Within the mountains lives a dangerous Force. It can only be described as a deceiving magical being that commands perhaps more power than even I myself do as a healing shaman. It is looking for you, Tien. You are said to posses the password to this spellbook. The Force will stop at nothing to coerce you to gain the password.

The Force wishes for the spellbook, because very soon the sun and the moon will appear in the sky together, for the first time in many centuries. This signifies the dawn of a new age. The one who possesses the spellbook at the time when both the sun and moon have risen their highest will begin the new age. If the Force has the spellbook at that time, it will have all the power it needs in order to cover our corner of the world in a deep, black darkness. This darkness will soon cause every man, woman and child to either perish at the hands of the Force, or succumb to its dark powers.

You, Tien, are the only one who may stop the Force, for you are said to possess the password to this spellbook. Once it has the book in its hands, the Force will not hesitate to torture you in *order to gain the password and open the spellbook.*

Now that I am gone, the village is no longer safe for you. Leave immediately, and follow the path into the Tien Shan Mountains to begin your search for the spellbook. I cannot say more now, but this will eventually lead you to your parents, if only you make the correct choices.

And finally, take heed of my words, Tien: you are in great danger, and you are alone. Accept help from those you believe you can trust; your judgment will not fail you. Remember that I love you, and although I cannot be with you at this time, I will always protect you.

Your Loving Godmother

As I read Wise Woman's note, I felt different emotions pass through my chest, leaving me quite weak by the end. Closing my eyes for a moment, I tried to imagine what my family would look like. I could see all of them, standing with me and smiling. They looked like me: the same skin, same eyes and same thick hair.

Before I could think more about a possible reunion with my family, a cold wind blew through the window, ruffling my hair. I opened my eyes, and saw Wise Woman's still body.

She looked calm, as though she had simply laid down for a quick rest and not gotten up yet. For the first time, I realized that I would never see Wise Woman again. Tears came to my eyes, washing away the happiness that had flooded me only minutes ago.

Forcing myself to turn away from Wise Woman, I

walked to the other end of her room and packed a small hand-woven bag with clothes, some food and an extra pair of sandals. I also packed a blanket. Slinging it over my shoulder, I was about to leave, when I heard voices.

Unfamiliar shadows loomed outside the hut, drawing closer at every moment. I watched from the window of the hut as they silently crossed the mud patch, where I had so often played as a child. I glanced at the door, and then back at Wise Woman, who lay still on the bed. I felt my heart begin to beat quickly as I leapt behind the large clay stove, from where I could see the room. I inhaled the smell of cooked rice and vegetables as the bamboo door creaked open.

A group of strange men entered the hut, murmuring among themselves. The black torches they held seemed to cloak the room in a fearsome, impenetrable darkness. These must be the men Wise Woman had mentioned. Fear flooded my veins, and I took a deep breath, attempting to steady my thumping heart as my body trembled against the rough reed wall.

The men looked at Wise Woman's still body. The leader of the group held his shining black torch in the air, and snapped his fingers. Flames sprang forth from the torch as though fueled by some mystical power. The other men followed suit. Then, laughing cruelly, they set their torches to her body. Flames licked her clothes, turning them black. Within moments, I had lost all sight of Wise Woman's body, the last memory I would ever have of her.

I cried out, forgetting my efforts to be hidden only

moments before. Leaping from my hiding spot onto the back of the leader, I beat my fists upon his head, screaming for help. To my surprise, a youthful voice sounded out as I beat down. I hesitated, wondering if the master of forces so powerful could be a young man only a few years older than me.

Sensing my surprise, the other men tried to grab me. I was too fast for them, and darted out of the hut, with the smell of smoke still in my throat. My eyes watering from the heat, I rushed down the path, hoping to get help from one of the villagers. The shouts of the mysterious leader followed me, ringing in my ears.

"Catch her! Run, fools!"

To my horror, other men burned down the village, one hut at a time. I stood in the center of the village, transfixed, watching my home vanish within the leaping flames. The faint cries of my fellow villagers as they tried in vain to escape the inferno that had enveloped their homes filled my ears. Then, with tears in my eyes, I ran from the men, and towards the snowcapped mountains.

Chapter Two

A New Friend—And a Guide

I tore down the familiar dirt road that led out of the village, my lungs burning as I turned to see the men following me, shouting out angrily. I stopped running at the fork in the road. The path to my right led to the next village, one I knew well from my trips with Wise Woman, on which she would heal those who suffered in other villages with her strange magic. To my left, the road became narrower, and wove endlessly into the black night. I looked up, and saw the Tien Shan Mountains mere miles away.

I stood still for a moment, my mind racing. Should I take the path to the next village and seek help? My hands

clutching the sack that held my belongings, I took an un-
certain step to the right. To my surprise, as I did so, I felt
my heart urge me in the other direction. Fear engulfed
me once more as I saw the band of men sprinting down
the path.

My heart in my throat, I leapt into thorny bushes,
feeling the brown branches scratch my arms. Trying to
suppress my frightened breathing and shaking hands, I
clutched my sack and the package Wise Woman had given
me. The men ran past me, their torches still burning. My
heart beat sounded loudly in my chest as my mind raced,
overwhelmed by the loss of Wise Woman.

I was unsure of what to do next. I waited until it was
completely dark before I set out to scale the mountain,
following the path Wise Woman had outlined for me. It
was slippery, covered with snow, and I almost fell twice,
but kept trudging upwards. The third time I slipped, I fell,
and slid into a bush on the side of the mountain. By then it
was daybreak. I struggled to get up, but the branches held
me prisoner. The dark night had begun to recede, taking
some of my fear with it.

I could now see the village huts far below me, blackened stubs in the distance. Snow weighed down the bare
branches of various bushes on the seldom used path. With
my eyes distracted by the new sights around me, I failed
to see a rock obstructing my path. With a loud cry, I toppled face first into the nearest bush. Sputtering, I wiped
the cold snow from my face, and flailed about in an unsuccessful attempt to free myself from the prickly branches.

With a sigh, I lay limp for a few moments, until a young man's voice said, "Here, let me help."

My eyes shot open. I looked around, but no one was there. I was worried, but bravely addressed the voice, "Show yourself!"

"All right, all right, I will."

A huge black owl nearly half my size landed next to the bush, fluttering its wings as it spoke. My mouth was wide open. I blinked once, then twice, to clear my vision. The bird was still there, looking at me. It had stripes under its eyes, making it look slightly sinister. The owl leaned in, squinting to get a closer look at me.

"Have you been crying?"

The curious, piping tone so like my own urged me to speak. Shocked, I said, "You're an owl."

"Yes." It raised an eyebrow, causing me to smile.

"A black owl...I've never seen one of those before!" I could not take my eyes off the strange animal for fear it would vanish.

The owl ruffled its feathers, and said, "I have many different forms. An owl is simply my preferred one. "

"And...you can talk!"

Suddenly, the owl fluttered its feather tips. As it did so, a strange ripple passed through the air, as though a giant hand was ripping fabric apart. The ripple enveloped the owl, covering its wings, then feet, and finally the soot-colored body and head. I watched as the creature sank into the ripple, and vanished. Blinking several times, I convinced myself that I had been hallucinating. Rolling sideways, I fell out of the bush onto the hard, icy ground.

With a twitter, the owl appeared in front of me, flapping its wings angrily.

"Well, there's gratitude for you. I go through all this trouble to show you one of my talents, and then you walk away!"

I shook my head, and looked at the owl, assuring myself that it was indeed real. Then, gathering my thoughts, I spoke in what I thought would be an adult manner.

"You didn't even change form…that's impossible to do. Besides, I have to be going."

The owl perched on my head, all signs of annoyance gone, and former curiosity returned.

"My name is Zharabi. Pleased to meet you."

The owl fluttered down to my shoulder, and held out a talon. I shook it, and then said hesitantly, "I'm Tien Ming. It's nice to meet you, Zharabi. But…just one question… how can you talk?"

Zharabi fluffed himself up importantly.

"Well, I used to live with a magician. He was an alchemist. I have three times the brain, powers, and lifespan of an ordinary owl. My caretaker died many years ago. For some time, I had no home, and aimlessly wandered among the mountains. A short while ago, however, I learned that my master was alive, so I came here looking for him."

"What made you think he was dead in the first place?" As soon as I had spoken, I regretted my question. Zharabi's eyes narrowed as he tried in vain to remember something. He waited a few moments before responding quietly, "I don't...nothing. It was a strange event..." He trailed off, clearly not wanting to speak of his master any longer. I couldn't think of anything to say, but luckily, Zharabi broke the awkward silence by changing the topic.

"And you? What brings you to wander the Tien Shan Mountains? They seem to be your namesake."

I sighed. Zharabi looked at me carefully, as though trying to read my mind.

"I'm...searching for something." I was unsure of how much to tell this stranger.

He looked at me for a moment, and then spoke softly.

"I can sense from looking at you that you have recently suffered a great shock, and horrible images are etched in your memory. A burning woman...crying out...a note... men...a burning village...running away...slipping." His voice was calm, and almost familiar.

As Zharabi spoke, I could feel the memories from the previous night washing over me. The pain was white hot. I cried out, and fell to the ground. I was shaking again, and writhing, as the memory of the men setting fire to Wise Woman came back, sharper than ever. I rolled over, and retched the remains of my last meal on the nearest bush. I felt my vision grow hazy, and my heart beat faster and faster.

As the images burned the insides of my eyes, I put my hands over my face, and said angrily, "No! Make it stop!"

The images vanished, and the insides of my eyes became black. I slowly opened them, and saw Zharabi gazing at me curiously through his large, dark eyes. I scooted away from him suspiciously, and asked, "Why can't you take human form?"

He shifted uneasily on his perch.

"I could...but it would be dangerous."

"Why?" I asked.

The owl only chuckled, and asked, "So what is this quest that you have been sent on?"

I was disappointed that Zharabi had not answered my question, but felt that I could trust him. I said, "I'm searching for a spellbook. I think it belonged to my family."

"Oh?" Zharabi's question was spoken lightly, but I sensed that he was surprised and intrigued.

As I opened my mouth to explain further, Zharabi spotted the lumpy package I was clutching. He eyed the package curiously.

"What's in there?"

I was taken aback for a moment when I saw the package, and a fresh wave of tears threatened to overcome me. With some difficulty, I pushed back my sadness and spoke.

"I-I don't know. Wise Woman gave the package to me. She said it would help me survive..." I trailed off. Zharabi nodded slowly.

"Well, it seems to me that you already have some sort of power that helps you do that. You have been given the grace of the mountains, Tien, which is no small honor. Now, open the package."

I slid to my knees, and put the package on the ground

in front of me. It was lumpy and soft, and as I ripped away the brown paper, I gasped at the sight that met my eyes.

It was a green *salwaar kameez*, a traditional Indian outfit, and one that I had seen trader's daughters wear sometimes, when their fathers came from India to trade valuable materials.

The material was fluid and soft, and the top had beautiful embroidery on it, of a willowy tree with waving branches and glittering leaves. Small green stones on the outfit winked and glittered in the morning sun.

A striking green hemmed strip of cloth and long, loose pants lay on top of the outfit. I knew from watching the tradesmen's daughters that the hemmed cloth was to be worn around my neck, or slung loosely around my shoulders. I picked up the outfit carefully. Zharabi didn't waste any time in ushering me toward the nearest covering of bushes.

"Change into it, and let's see how you look."

I hurried behind a large gathering of leafy bushes, and slipped into the tunic and pants. As I wore it, I felt a sudden change within me. I looked down, and saw, to my immense surprise, that the embroidery was glowing brighter then ever in the sun. The day no longer felt crisp or cold, but pleasantly warm. My fears were gone, replaced by a new confidence and pride. I was jolted out of my admiration of the clothing by Zharabi's voice.

"Tien, look at this!"

I hurried out from behind the bush, and found Zharabi picking at the brown paper with his beak. A secret pocket was revealed in the seemingly flimsy packing, and within it was jewelry. Pure gold bangles, earrings, and an anklet lay glimmering among the folds of brown paper. I bent down, and scooped up the jewelry in my hands. It had clearly been carefully crafted and seemed almost new. I put on the jewelry without thinking. Zharabi watched me, a strange look on his face, as though he were trying to place something.

"Tien, the necklace is missing..." He frowned, and his face contorted while he tried to remember something.

"Why would the necklace be missing?" I sighed. Was this a part of my past...or just a mere coincidence?

Zharabi broke the silence.

"We might find it later...but for now, we should leave. Whoever you're running from could be here anytime soon."

I nodded. I spun around, and the outfit followed my body. My feet were clad in the simple bamboo sandals that Wise Woman had made for me long ago. Zharabi twittered as I spun; something I took to be a laugh. Then, spotting my old ragged clothes, he spoke once more.

"We need to hide your clothes."

"All right."

I bent down, and gathered up the clothes. Depositing them and the brown packaging in a ditch by the bush, I covered it up with soil, and patted the earth down. No one would be able to tell that something was hidden there. When I was done, Zharabi fluttered to my shoulder, and roosted there.

"It's nice to sit on a human shoulder again." Zharabi sighed. I smiled. He smiled back at me and said quietly, "I'd like to come with you, and help you solve your riddle. It would be an honor."

I nodded and replied, "I could make do with a guide, Zharabi."

"Not just a guide, Tien, but a friend too."

As we continued to walk down the mountain path, I looked back at my former home, and saw a single spire of smoke rise from the village. I could have sworn I saw men clad in black moving among the dying flames, but I simply turned my back on my old life, and took steps toward my new one.

NOT LONG AFTER Tien and Zharabi had disappeared around a distant curve in the winding mountain path, men stomped up the path, trailing ashes, their leader seething. In the daylight, their torches seemed much less menacing. Suddenly, the leader held up his hand. The men stopped, and were silent as their commander strode to the bush where Tien had changed. He stood quite still for a moment, then bent down, and recovered her clothes from the pile of earth, a distasteful expression upon his face.

"Sir, is something wrong?"

"They were here. Take these." The leader shoved the clothes into one of the men's hands.

"Get rid of those. We will not follow the girl—she will come to us. I want half of you to go smother any remains of the fire and to hide any traces that someone started it. Be quick, and return by nightfall." The voice from within the mask was youthful, but the eyes that peered out were dark with a strange mystical power.

Half the men bowed respectfully, and hurried down the mountain path, the torches hanging limply at their sides. The other half waited for orders, their backs rigid as they stood in the morning sun. The leader snapped his slim fingers, and the wind began to blow fiercely.

There was movement in the air, marking the arrival of an invisible but powerful being. Without a word, the leader stepped forward, and vanished into the air. The men followed him. When all of the men had disappeared, the wind began to blow once more. When it stopped, all signs of the strange distortion were gone.

Only footprints in the snow remained.

Chapter Three

The Golden Pass

"So where are we going?" I asked Zharabi.

It was several days later. The sun shone brightly upon the mountains, and despite myself, I couldn't help but feel pleased. Our journey had gone well so far, and the events following Wise Woman's death felt distant, and as though they had belonged to another world entirely.

"The Golden Pass." Zharabi consistently fluttered a few feet ahead of me, rarely resting on my shoulders. He had an endless wealth of knowledge of the mountains and their mysterious magic, which he was more than happy to share with me.

"Why is it called the Golden Pass?"

"Years ago, golden snow leopards used to rule these areas of the Himalayas. They were taken care of by the sorcerer who ruled over the mountains. The sorcerer later built the Golden Pass to allow the magical leopards to cross into the Tien Shan Mountain Range—that's where we are headed."

"Will we find the spellbook there?"

As before, when I had mentioned the spellbook to Zharabi, his tone became light, but it was clearer than ever that he was hiding his true feelings about it. I remembered how he had related the tale of his master, an alchemist, to me. Remembering that my grandfather had been an alchemist, I wondered if he could have been Zharabi's master, but did not trust my new companion enough to ask.

"Finding the spellbook will be difficult," said Zharabi. "There are not many places where it could be…but there is a magical being that may possess it. The Force will protect it to the death."

"The Force?" I asked Zharabi. "How do you know about the Force?"

"Every magical creature is aware of the Force," Zharabi informed me. "We fear the dark spell it casts over these mountains…If the Force possesses the spellbook, it will bode ill for all of us. How did you come to hear of such sinister magic?"

"My guardian told me," I replied, unsure of how much more I should reveal.

Zharabi was intrigued, however, and continued to

press the topic.

"Who was your guardian?"

"Wise Woman," I said. "She was one of the Elders in the village nearest to these mountains."

"Wise Woman...She is very powerful, isn't she?"

"What do you mean?" I asked.

"Her name," Zharabi explained to me, "reveals great power and wealth of knowledge. She must have known Sangmu," he murmured as an addition.

"Sangmu?" I glanced at Zharabi, who seemed lost in thought; it was several moments before he responded.

"She was the last Sorceress of the Himalayas," he said quietly, as though the subject was one that could not be spoken of.

"What did she do for the mountains while she was sorceress?" I was still in awe of the magical world which I had stepped into only days ago.

"She created the Golden Pass."

"You didn't mention that before," I said. "Where is she now?"

Zharabi shook his head in response. "No one knows... She vanished." He flew on ahead of me, and I understood that I was not to ask any more questions of the great Sorceress. My thoughts soon returned to my family and the mysterious spellbook, both of which seemed far more difficult to find now than they had back in Wise Woman's hut while I read her note.

I realized that when I thought of my family now, no visions of a future life with Wise Woman came along with it. I felt the grim truth press upon me like a weight, as I understood that my childish notions had already begun to vanish; I was growing up...Would I even want a family at the end of my journey?

"We're here." Zharabi's voice brought me back to the present.

At first, I could not see the entrance to the pass. A large cliff loomed in front of us, its gray mass casting an ominous shadow upon the shimmering white snow. A small crevice in the rock, no taller or wider than myself, was the only entrance. I walked past Zharabi, and looked into the pass. Long icicles hung precariously from the ceiling, dripping onto the snow below, appearing as frightening monsters in the gloom of the passage. Even the snow looked dull within the Golden Pass. My skin prickled as I looked into the blank, endless tunnel. Wind blew through the passage, buffeting Zharabi back a few inches. Holding up a hand to shield myself, I walked into the small opening.

Our progress through the tunnel was slow. I used my hands to carefully feel the cold, smooth sides of the passage so as to not trip and fall. We were soon plunged into complete darkness. Although my eyes were open, I could not see anything; it felt as though I were blind.

Suddenly, a strange clicking noise echoed through the tunnel. I whipped around, and strained my eyes through the shadows to search for whatever was following us.

Zharabi and I remained still for several moments, listening. My heart beat loudly inside my chest, but I felt a strange excitement rise from within me, causing me to tremble. The sound came again, this time followed by a low, menacing growl. I could barely make out Zharabi as he swooshed past me to search the tunnel behind us. I listened as his wings beat through the air, the quiet swishing sounding terribly loud in the suspenseful silence.

Suddenly, the tunnel fell silent, and I heard the shrill screech of an owl. I could not move for the fear that filled my body. More growls echoed in the passageway, and then the clacking noise came my way, but with shorter intervals this time. With a start, I realized that it was not a horse's hoof against the stone floor that had made the strange noise, but a beast's claw.

I started to run blindly through the tunnel, tripping over my own feet several times. My breath came in short, frightened gasps. Without warning, I tripped on something cold, and fell face first. I felt my face burn as the snow melted against my warm cheeks. I crawled through the snow, shivering from fear and the cold, and far too afraid to look behind me.

To my relief, a small opening in the roof of the tunnel allowed me to dimly view the widening of the Golden Pass. I quickly scrambled to my feet, and struggled through the snow. From behind me, a roar echoed through the tunnel. I spun around, and gasped.

A leopard unlike any other stood less than five feet away from me. Although the light was dim, I was able to see the animal quite clearly. It was as large as I was, and had amber eyes that glowed with concentrated anger. The golden coat of the leopard gave off its own glow in the weak light. I was stunned speechless by the beast that stood in front of me; I had only heard of magical golden snow leopards in ancient legends, but never dreamed that they would actually exist.

The leopard ran through the snow effortlessly, quickly closing the gap between us. I stood stock still, an impending feeling of doom rising slowly in my chest. I had given up on ever seeing Zharabi again, when a huge eagle swept me up, its talons crushing my chest.

I screamed and kicked and hit it with my sack, as the eagle carried me effortlessly through the large tunnel, its body mass nearly as large as a group of several small huts.

"Tien, it's me! Stop it!"

I looked up, and saw the dark feathers of a large eagle. As it glanced down at me, I saw the large, dark eyes, and the familiar circles that lined them.

"Zharabi?"

"Yes! Climb up onto my back. We have to get out of here!" Zharabi's wings beat furiously as he spoke to me, carrying us swiftly through the endless dark tunnel.

I scrambled up onto the eagle's back, and slung my sack over my chest for safekeeping. Zharabi's wings pounded as we raced through the tunnel. A strange rush of adrenaline ran through my body as I gripped the eagle's soft, velvety feathers. I could not see where we going, for we had been plunged into complete and total blackness. The tunnel seemed to go on forever, and although I was worried about what would happen if we didn't find the way out, my excitement at the sheer pace of our flight quelled all other emotions.

Suddenly, Zharabi veered sharply to the right, and began to spiral downwards so quickly that I nearly slid off his back. I quickly snatched a hold of the feathers, and pulled myself tightly against them. We curved haphazardly underneath a huge rock formation, and continued to hurtle through the endless passage.

Snow and icicles showered us as we banged the sides of the tunnel. At one point, it became so narrow that Zharabi was forced to compress his wings and beat them, a painful feat.

I saw a faint light at the end of tunnel, which had begun to widen again. Zharabi stretched his wings, and put on one final burst of speed.

We tumbled out of the tunnel onto a snow-covered path. He dropped me to the ground, and I leapt up even as the cold snow began to burn on my bare arms. Zharabi faltered for a moment, and then I saw the leopard again. It was panting slightly, but otherwise seemed relatively calm. For a moment, no one moved or spoke; the only sound around us was that of the wind whistling between the bare branches of the numerous tiny bushes that lay scattered amongst the snow, brown blemishes upon the pure white surface.

Finally, the leopard broke the tense silence. Slowly sinking to the snow, it bowed to both of us.

Zharabi was confused. "Why are you bowing to us?"

His voice was commanding and strong, but I could sense fear within it.

"I'm not bowing to you, shapeshifter." The leopard sounded amused as she spoke.

"Why are you bowing to her?" Zharabi continued to be on his guard.

The leopard bowed once more, its magnificent paws scraping against the icy snow, and said quietly, "Because she commands the grace of the mountains."

Chapter Four

Daya

Zharabi broke the silence. There was a poof, and he reappeared as a black owl once more. Settling on my shoulder, he said in a quieter voice, "You may not have meant us harm, but you gave us a good scare down there in the Golden Pass."

The leopard looked away. "I'm sorry. I have to be more careful now. Once upon a time, kindness was accepted in the world, but these days, shadows lurk in every corner, and one can never be too careful…especially in these mountains."

I could clearly see that the leopard was a girl. She did not have any distinct markings, but the glow that emanated off her reminded me that she was indeed magical. There was something lurking in her heart, her very soul, that was causing her pain every day. I wanted to ask what it was, but she approached and spoke again before I could say anything.

"My name is Daya. I am one of the few remaining golden snow leopards left."

Zharabi snorted.

"And what would an owl like you know of these matters?" Daya turned on Zharabi, her amber eyes suddenly glowing pools of fire. Then, as though deciding that it was not necessary to argue, she spoke to me instead.

"I'm sorry, and would like to offer my service to you in whatever quest you may be on, because I know the Himalayas very well. These mountains are my home."

Zharabi hesitated then spoke, "Well, you seem nice enough...I'm Zharabi, and this is..."

"I'm Tien Ming."

"It's nice to meet the two of you."

Daya looked at me, and I got the same feeling that I had gotten with Zharabi. It was as though she was trying to read my mind. Daya looked at me, and then turned away.

"I am sorry about Wise Woman." Her voice was thick with emotion. "My father was also taken from me at a young age by..." She faltered here, and I saw the pain rise from her heart to her eyes. They looked glassy, as though she could no longer see through them. Then, she spoke in a voice so quiet that we had to lean forward to hear it.

"...by humans."

She bent down, and said softly, "I tried to kill a human, a long time ago."

Daya began to walk slowly on the snow, away from the Golden Pass. I kept pace with her, while Zharabi fluttered in the air around us.

"It was night. The stars were out, and I was suffering. My father had been killed, killed by his own evil…maybe human's evil as well. I don't know. I only know the pain I felt. It was a white-hot burning inside of me. I vowed to kill the next human I set eyes on, to avenge my father's death. I realize now how foolish I was, how death cannot be avenged by murder. I tried to kill a young woman. I realized that even in my anger, I was not able to hurt her."

Daya continued, "Then, when I had been about to kill her, a man appeared. He wounded me with his sword, and I was forced to leave.

I was still.

My voice shook slightly when I spoke. "I-I'm her daughter. I'm Rani's daughter…the woman's daughter."

"You look like her." Daya smiled momentarily.

Then, lowering her voice respectfully, she said, "I'm sorry, Tien. Your mother is dead." Her smile faded, disappearing like the rays of the dying sun.

I said with more confidence than I felt, "Wise Woman sent me to find my parents. They can't be dead. But even if they weren't alive, I have no home to return to."

My stomach lurched as I said this, unrelated to the wild ride through the tunnel.

Daya thought for a moment and then said, "I can take you to the sacred grove in the Himalayas. It might help you find what you are looking for."

"The spellbook," I said to her. "I'm looking for the spellbook."

Daya turned to look at me, her expression unreadable. Then, she said quietly, "I see...I will help you, because I am also searching for the book, and the Force that may possess it."

"Why?" I asked.

"I want to kill the Force, because it destroyed my breed with its dark power."

Daya then turned to Zharabi and asked, "And what about you? What do you want with the spellbook?"

"I do not want the spellbook," said Zharabi. "I want to destroy the Force to avenge my master, who was taken by it."

A contemptuous look crossed Daya's face, and she opened her mouth to speak scathingly, but then seemed to think the better of it.

Instead she said, "We must hurry, because it will start to snow soon...stay close. The Himalayas are not as safe as they seem."

Daya turned, and padded through the snow. I watched her traverse a barely visible path under and around the maze created by rocks that jutted out from underneath the snow, looking like sharp teeth.

I glanced at Zharabi, who seemed to be pondering the ominous warning. I sighed, and followed Daya, while Zharabi trailed behind. We soon vanished into the crevices of the mountains.

Chapter Five

A Sign of Evil

My journey through the mountains continued without much incident. We ascended the Himalayan Mountains, with white snow surrounding us like a blanket wrapping an infant. The path that had led us to the Golden Pass continued to weave through the mountain peaks, twisting and turning more times than I could count. Every night, we stopped to rest, and ate what little food Daya could scavenge. Although it was not a life anything similar to the one I had led with Wise Woman, I found myself happier than I had ever been.

Finally the grueling path we had been following ended. The sun shone brightly in the sky, reflecting off snow that covered the path. We had struggled to climb a large hill, and I could barely breathe because of the stitch in my side. Suddenly, Daya, who had been leading the way, stopped short. I took the break gladly, and collapsed into the snow, panting.

"What's the matter?" Zharabi flew over me to Daya. Looking out from atop the hill, he eyed the endless rolling mountaintops dusted with snow, and the sun that poured light upon them. Looking down the hill, Zharabi turned to Daya.

"What should we do?"

When Daya did not respond, my curiosity was aroused. Standing up, I brushed the snow off of my clothes, and trudged over to the top of the hill. Beneath us was more fresh, untouched snow. At the bottom of the hill was a large cave, whose mouth leered unpleasantly at me. Behind the cave lay only a few feet of snow before the ground ended into a deep abyss. I could see a wooden bridge stretching across the ravine, loosely attached to the next mountain peak. I looked at Daya.

"What's the problem? We can just cross the bridge. Isn't that the way we are headed anyways?"

She nodded. "It's not the bridge that worries me. What will happen when we cross it?"

"I don't understand…" I trailed off, and turned to Zharabi for an explanation. He looked uneasy.

"Daya is right. There is something about the ravine that seems dangerous. Perhaps if we wait until night whatever is in there will not see us cross."

"It's the cave that seems scary to me," I muttered under my breath. Daya and Zharabi did not hear me.

"I think we should cross now," said Daya. "We have no guarantee that we won't be seen during the night. This way we can at least fight."

Zharabi shrugged, his disagreement visible by the expression on his face. Flapping his wings, he swooped down the hill. Daya let out a growl of annoyance, and followed him.

I hesitated for a few moments at the top of the hill. I didn't know if we should go near the cave at all. The more I thought about it, the less I wanted to be anywhere near the mouth of the cave. Its black emptiness taunted me, and the mouth sneered even as I watched.

As Daya passed by the cave, snow began to move in flurries around her. She deftly leapt out of the way, but it continued to follow her. I watched, my eyes narrowed, as the snow suddenly took the form of another leopard with ice-blue eyes. Daya roared, and raised her paw to strike down the formation of snow, but the other leopard jumped out of the way. Fixating its eyes on the snow, it growled. I gasped as the snow began to stiffen and turn blue; it was becoming ice. Daya began to lose her footing, and started to slide towards the ravine.

Sliding down the hill on the slippery ice, I skidded across the ice towards Daya. As I shot past the white leopard, it took a swipe at me, and I rolled out of the way just in time. Drawing nearer to the edge, I realized that I hadn't thought of a way to secure myself before rescuing

Daya. My heart sank; and I looked around hoping to find something to hold on to.

Daya was now struggling to hold on to the edge of the cliff with her two front paws. Her amber eyes were wide with fear as she slipped further over the edge. Reaching my arm out, I grabbed her paw.

"Hold on!" I scooted back across the ice, pulling Daya up slowly. Suddenly, the wind began to blow fiercely, blowing snow through the air. I turned in time to see the other leopard leap through the air towards me. I raised a hand to shield myself, but it was too late; the leopard landed on top of me, its weight bearing down upon me. I looked into the icy blue eyes, and found myself looking at the young man that I had beaten the night of Wise Woman's death, his dark, penetrating eyes staring into my own.

Suddenly, the claws of the leopard sunk into my chest. I opened my hand, and felt Daya's paw slip. My heart plummeted as I thought of her falling into the ravine.

"Who are you? What do you want? We are just travelers." I tried to sit up, but the leopard pressed down on me once more, its claws digging further into my clothes.

"Travelers! I find that difficult to believe. An owl, snow leopard, and a young girl traveling through the dark wilderness of the Himalaya Mountains is unheard of. Humans fear this side of the mountain because of its dark power—they do not dare to encroach upon what is not theirs."

My left hand was beginning to grow numb from

holding Daya's paw. I could faintly hear her scraping against the rock as she attempted to find footing to climb up. I continued to try to distract the leopard.

"We have the right to walk these mountains. They are not yours alone. And the owl and the snow leopard are my friends."

"Friends do not come from those who are not of your own kind," snapped the leopard. "Everyone only befriends those who are similar to them. It would seem to me that you have not been drawn to these strange creatures for friendship—but perhaps for power."

" I have no power. I am only a traveler. Let me go."

The leopard bent close to me, its eyes boring into mine.

"Do you know what the punishment for wandering into these lands is, traveler?"

Without waiting for an answer, the leopard growled, "Death."

Raising a paw, the leopard threw its head back and roared, the wind whipping snow faster and faster as it did so. My eyes widened, and I found that although my mouth was open, I could no longer speak for the fear that flooded my body.

Then out of the whirling wind came Daya, knocking the other leopard to the ground. Raising her paw, she struck it across its face. No blood rushed from the wound; instead, snow fell away from its face, leaving part of the leopard's body missing.

"Go back to where you came from, golden leopard!

Do not break the ancient laws of your kind!" snarled the white leopard, its words echoing strangely in the wind.

I watched as Daya raised her paw a second time, but hesitated at her opponent's words. She soon lost her chance to destroy the beast as more snow replaced the leopard's cheek, and it scrambled out from under Daya, panting slightly.

"Tien, we must make it across the bridge." A voice in my ear made me start. Turning, I saw Zharabi through the snow and wind, beckoning me with his wing.

"Where were you?" I began to crawl across the ice, Zharabi alongside me.

"I helped Daya get her footing, and remained hidden. Be silent."

I heeded his command, and for several moments the only noise was the whistling of wind as it blew fiercely. Finally, I saw the bridge looming in front of me, a skeleton of wooden planks precariously hanging across the ravine. I stood up, and stepped onto the bridge. I could feel the tremors as I tiptoed across the thin wooden planks. Zharabi remained by my side as we slowly crossed the bridge.

A roar sounded through the wind. I turned.

"Daya!" I ran back across the bridge, but Zharabi flew in front of me.

"Tien, no! We have to cross the bridge. Come on!" He urged me in the opposite direction, but another roar, this time louder, sounded through the snowstorm. I made up my mind. Running across the last few feet of the bridge, I fell to my knees and packed snow into a tiny ball.

Then, scrambling over to the nearest bush, I snapped off the largest branch. Turning, I ran back across the bridge. The wooden planks shook as I ran, and began to snap behind me. I made a running leap onto the ice at the end of the bridge just as the last wooden plank snapped, leaving only two ropes behind.

I used my elbows to push myself across the ice, leaving the broken bridge behind me. In front of me, blurry through the howling wind, I could see the shape of the cave, and the hill that I had slid down earlier. As I crawled slowly along the ice, I was careful not to move to my right, for fear that I would fall into the ravine. Finally, I came in contact with something soft and furry.

"Daya?" She murmured something in response.

"She's hurt." Zharabi was on my right now, examining Daya.

"We have to get her out of here. Come on, help me."

I grabbed Daya's paws, and began to slide back across the ice, towards the broken bridge. The wind was slowing now; in fact, it had almost stopped. I hoped that the strange leopard was gone. I reached the bridge, and rolled Daya carefully onto the ropes that were left.

"That won't work," said Zharabi impatiently. Twirling in the air, a ripple ran through his body, enlarging him until he was my size.

"Wait for me here. I'll take her to the other side first, and then come back for you." Carefully picking up Daya in his beak, Zharabi flapped his wings and soared under the bright blue sky to the other side of the ravine.

A noise behind me made me turn around. There was nothing on the ice, but I could sense that I was not alone. Suddenly, a ripple in the air moved towards me, barreling across the ice. My eyes widened, and I leapt onto the ropes of the bridge, one foot on each rope. They shook, and I slipped and fell through the ropes. Grabbing the ropes with my hands just in time, I dangled precariously in the air above the ravine for several moments, my heart beating quickly. Moving my hands along the rope, I began to slowly cross to the other side.

Looking back, I saw the ripple darken, and could see that it was actually a sphere as large as Wise Woman's hut. What was it? I felt my heart stop as I remembered the Force Wise Woman had told me about. This must be the evil magical being. My hands trembling, I moved them even faster along the rope. I could see Zharabi carefully setting Daya down on the other side of the ravine. It seemed terribly far, and I could feel my arms aching from the effort of pulling my weight along the ropes.

"Stop! Do not move any further!" A voice from behind me called out angrily. I did not turn around; it was the same voice as the leopard.

"Tien, stop! Do not be foolish."

I wondered with another, new leap of fear how the shapeshifter knew my name. Wise Woman had been right; there was danger all around me. I swung along the rope, but was only halfway across it when I heard a snap. Behind me, the men that had burned my village had cut the rope. I screamed as I swung towards the cliff face in front of me. The icicles and cold blue walls loomed closer and closer. I heard the laughter of the men echoing in the ravine around me. With the wind whistling past my ears, I wrapped my legs around the rope, and held out my hand to the approaching wall, hoping to save myself from being impaled on an icicle.

As I swung into the wall, I grabbed a protruding rock, and pushed myself away from the wall. Without looking at the men, I began to climb up the rope, holding the wall for support. The dark shadow of a large bird loomed above me; it comforted me to know that Zharabi was overhead, even if he was far away. My feet still clinging to the rope, I clenched my teeth, and began to slowly climb up the side of the ravine, using the various protruding rocks to slowly pull myself along. Finally, after what seemed like years, I reached the top of the ravine. Zharabi was once more a slightly over-large owl, and he used his beak to help pull me onto the snow. I lay still for a few moments, my face only inches from the snow, breathing deeply. Turning around, I saw the men standing in a line on the other side of the ravine, the snow-white leopard among them.

"Why aren't they coming after us?" I panted. Zharabi replied, "They cannot enter this area of the mountain because it is where the sacred bamboo grove lies. They have only breached it once before, when Sangmu had fled, taking Rinzen with her."

"What is Rinzen? Why were they able to breach it when Sangmu had gone?" As before, I felt a strange rush of excitement when the name of Sangmu was mentioned;

the simple word seemed laced with power, and I was intrigued by it.

"Rinzen was the flower that Sangmu created during her time as Sorceress. It protected all magical creatures under her rule, and stopped the dark forces from penetrating this sacred area. If any creature was ever in danger, the grove was the one place where they would always be safe."

"Why did she leave?" I asked. "What made her run from the mountains?"

Zharabi responded calmly, "It is difficult to say...there are not many clues left behind to tell the tale. Sangmu simply fled, taking her beloved Rinzen with her. After her disappearance, the creatures of the mountains were no longer protected, and the Force was able to breach the grove—I'm assuming the purpose was to find the book."

He took a deep breath, and continued, "The spellbook was always kept here in the grove, by Sangmu's side. She had acquired it some years previously from an alchemist's home, and seemed determined to protect it. Although I never saw the book, I knew that she kept it with her at all times to ensure that the Force would not be able to take it. Once she left, however, the book was unprotected...It may still be in the grove, but there is also a chance that the Force has taken it."

I opened my mouth to ask in which part of the mountains the Force's realm lay, but at that moment Daya groaned behind us.

Almost instantly forgetting my question, I hurried

over to Daya. Across her paws she had several cuts , which were glowing silver in the bright sunlight. I bent down and said, "Daya, I'm really sorry but I don't think I can carry you. Can you walk to the grove? Zharabi said it's only a short distance from here."

Daya opened her eyes, and nodded slowly. Raising her majestic head from the ground, she tried to lift up her body, but fell back onto the snow, wincing. Alarmed, I took her two front paws, and placed her upper body on my back.

"Here, help me. I don't think she'll be able to walk otherwise. Can you help her when we get to the grove?" I waited while Zharabi transformed into a large white horse as pale as the snow, with a rippling, silky mane and tail that shimmered in the midday sun.

I lifted Daya onto the stallion's back, and it whinnied, the dark eyes calm and still. I clambered on, holding Daya in front of me. The horse asked, "Ready?" I nodded.

White, feathery wings sprouted from either side of the horse, nearly twice my size. They beat rhythmically, and we rose above the mountain peaks, soaring over the untouched white landscape. I breathed in deeply, amazed at the sheer beauty of the snow-covered Himalayas. Soon I could see a small circle of green on the highest peak. We descended, and the air blew my hair back from my face, refreshing me. We landed outside the grove, and I could see a low rock wall surrounding the tall bamboo trees that waved in the slight breeze. Leaving Zharabi behind as he helped Daya, I stepped over the rock wall, and into the sacred bamboo grove.

Chapter Six

The Grove

I hesitantly walked through the bamboo trees, the patterns made by the sunlight through the forest reflected across my face and arms. Many different small paths wove through the thicket of trees.

Their green leaves were vibrant; everything seemed to be twice as alive within the grove. As I breathed in the sweet smell of bamboo and closed my eyes, I could feel myself falling under the spell of the grove. Around me, birds of colors I had never seen flitted around the trees in small circles, twittering.

Pushing aside branches that blocked my view of the clearing in the center of the grove, I stepped out onto a smooth, flat slab of rock. Its gray mass stretched out to the edge of the grove, where pure white marble formed a wall. I stepped out from the shade of the bamboo, and walked across the clearing, passing a large meditation rock on the way. I stopped at the rock, and stood in its shadow for a moment.

The large rock was shaded by a neem tree, whose large, weathered brown trunk stood deeply rooted next to the rock. Its branches were thick and strong, and stretched directly over the rock, their green leaves and pink flowers moving in the gentle breeze.

Red, blue, and yellow birds circled the tree, while others twittered within, hidden from my view. Steps that seemed to have been carved from the rock itself led to the top. I scampered up them, feeling like a young child again, back in my home village. I could almost imagine Wise Woman running behind me, scolding gently. At the top, I pushed up the branches of the neem tree, and found that I could see the entire range of the Himalayas, stretched out in front me as a shimmering landscape of snow and gray mountain peaks.

As I looked out among them, I felt truly at home for the first time since Wise Woman's death. I was suddenly able to view my quest for the spellbook as a more serious matter; things seemed to take on a new perspective.

I was amazed by the grove. Running down the stairs, I ran to the edge of the wall, and looked over it. Beneath me the steep slope of rock continued, until it blended in with the base of the nearest mountain. It was a wonderful sight. I turned to look at Daya and Zharabi, my head miraculously cleared.

Zharabi spoke up, in a worried tone, "Tien, we have some bad news."

Daya stepped in here. Her voice was also worried.

"We searched the hut for the spellbook, but instead we found this."

Zharabi spat out a single thing from his beak. It was a black torch.

Chapter Seven

Disunity

I looked at the smooth, black torch. It appeared to be made of marble, but was surprisingly light to hold. At the top, the torch curved slightly, leaving a hollow from which I presumed fire would erupt. The black marble, however, was smooth and untouched, not scarred from fire as I had expected.

I said quietly, "This is the same torch I saw that day. I remember it. The men dressed in black burned Wise Woman's body with these torches."

Zharabi said nothing, but took the torch from me, and dropped it in a hole in the ground.

As she looked at the torch, I saw Daya's eyes flicker

with the remembrance of something from her past. Drawing her gaze from the coal black torch to my face, Daya remained motionless for many moments. I asked her, "What's wrong?" At the sound of my voice, Daya quickly backed away, her paws making little noise.

"I should go. It is not my place to help you." Her voice contained fear, and—was it possible? Anger. I stepped forward to speak to Daya, but a derisive snort from Zharabi stopped me.

"I knew it."

Daya watched Zharabi as he began to cover up the torch with dirt once more. As he kicked the fine dirt over the torch with his claws, Zharabi snapped at Daya, "Well, get going then. We will just manage without you."

Daya laughed mirthlessly. "You need me! I alone know one of the only other locations where the spellbook may be...the Ghost Monastery."

"The Ghost Monastery?" As I spoke, the words sent shivers down my spine.

Zharabi replied, "It is on the other side of the mountain, but few dare to go there, for the Force's magic reigns absolute. It is there that the spellbook is kept, protected so that none may take it before the unity of the sun and the moon. But," his tone grew slightly derisive here, "we can find better help elsewhere."

A low growl came from Daya's throat. "What is that supposed to mean?"

"As if you don't know! We can simply find Rinzen, and uncover the map within it to find the Force's lair...

the Ghost Monastery!"

Daya growled again. "How do you know of Rinzen?"

Zharabi snorted. "Who doesn't know of Rinzen? Sangmu was the greatest sorceress of the mountains! Her soul was known to every magical being."

Daya had remained still, but slowly drew back as Zharabi fell silent.

In response, he shouted angrily across the clearing, "I knew trusting you was a mistake right from the start!"

"And why was that?" Daya's voice was barely a whisper, but anger was evident through her glowing amber eyes.

Zharabi was undeterred by her fury. "Snow leopards and other beasts of the mountains could never be trusted when humans came into play, because you always thought that you were better than the rest of us! You and your stupid rules and laws that segregate one breed from another are ridiculous."

"Don't talk about things you do not understand, Zharabi." Daya took several paces towards Zharabi now, the hackles on her back raised ever so slightly. Her tail flicked with irritation.

"Those laws were made by my father, who was king of these mountains and the area surrounding them. I must follow them." Daya turned to leave once more. I watched her go, confused as to why she was leaving. I glanced at Zharabi. He finished covering the torch with dirt, then called after Daya, "Those rules have not been followed for centuries. This is a new age now, where those of us dissimilar by feature must unite under a similar cause."

Daya stopped at the edge of the clearing, and responded flatly, "Man and beast are as separate as two races. They can never mix."

I felt cold fury rush through my body as I finally understood why Daya was leaving: because she believed that I, as a human, was not good enough to be in her presence.

"Look at me, Daya!" The anger in my voice must have been fierce, because Daya turned around to face me.

"I defy your rules and laws. I am a human of mixed race, with no proper tradition to call my own. I have no race and no family, yet I am not impure or different."

Zharabi added, "We all want something within the Ghost Monastery. Tien wants the spellbook to bring her family back to life, you want the spellbook away from the Force so that you might keep your kingdom within the mountains, and I want to destroy the Force to free my master from its prison."

Daya stood silent as a slight breeze stole through the grove, whispering as though it contained deep secrets.

I said quietly, "The dissimilarities among us do not matter if we have a common goal: to destroy the Force."

Daya hesitated, and took a single step towards us. Then, shaking her head, she stepped further back.

"I-I cannot turn against my people's beliefs. To do so would be treachery." She vanished between the towering bamboo shoots. I looked at Zharabi helplessly. He shouted after Daya, "Then you have already committed treachery, by spending time in our presence. You didn't seem so hesitant outside the Golden Pass, or when we saved your life!"

Daya continued walking. Zharabi yelled after her, "In turning your back on the one chance to avenge your breed, you are committing treachery!"

His words echoed across the mountains ominously. Moments after the echoes began to die away, Daya sprang out from the bamboo shoots towards the meditation rock. As she reached out to swipe at Zharabi, he changed form. The black feathers turned to smooth fur, and the dark eyes became large and round. Zharabi was now a black panther.

"Fool shapeshifter!" Daya landed deftly on the ground after her leap, and climbed up the meditation rock, where Zharabi sat watching her, his tail twitching ever so slightly, the black fur gleaming in the warm sun.

"Don't get angry at me," he said in a voice of dead calm. "You know as well as I do that when the sun and the moon join, all power will go to the Force if it possesses the spellbook." Standing up, Zharabi jumped down, step by step, until he stood by me.

I asked him, "What do you mean, 'when the sun and the moon join'?"

"It's something to do with balance of power, and..." Zharabi stopped short as Daya spoke.

"You want to understand?" She called down from the meditation rock. I glanced at Zharabi, who smiled at me, his white fangs bright and clean. I turned to Daya and nodded.

"Then follow me." With another single bound, she was back at the edge of the clearing, then beyond my sight as she passed into the bamboo. Crossing my arms, I frowned. I felt a ripple in the air next to me, and knew that Zharabi had changed into his preferred form once more. As the black owl settled on my shoulder, he asked, "Do you think we can trust her?"

Shrugging, I began to follow Daya. "We'll have to— it's the quickest way."

Chapter Eight

The Dark Rider

We traveled through the mountains for several days in silence until Daya finally spoke again.

"We are almost there. It is time for me to tell you the story of how the Force was created."

Without waiting for a response from Zharabi or me, she began.

"A long, long time ago, there was an ancient wizard, or Sorceress of the Mountains, who wished to somehow unite the Himalaya and Tien Shan ranges. She was very powerful, and managed to create the Golden Pass. With the creation of this magnificent tunnel, however, came problems. The sun and the moon were no longer happy.

For centuries before the pass had been created, the sun and moon had ruled over the world at the same time, side by side. This had been possible because although the moon represented dark and the sun represented light, there had been a balance between dark and light forces on earth. Thus, there had been no need for a quarrel among the two celestial bodies, and the sun and the moon were able to coexist in the sky, at peace with one another."

"When the Golden Pass had been created, a Force had come out of it, one that was dark and dangerous. Not only was it a shapeshifter, but it also possessed many powers that no wizard would ever have. The Force possessed the power to control the natural energies of the mountain. At first, the Sorceress of the Mountains was able to control this dangerous magical power, because it had not yet learned to think for itself. Soon, however, the Force realized that it could control its own power, and it broke free of the Sorceress of the Mountains, who fled. Because there was no longer a balance of good and evil, the sun and the moon could no longer rule together. The sun took the first twelve hours of the day, and the moon the second twelve. As we know it today, the balance of these powers changes seasonally. All clear so far?"

Daya turned to look at me. I nodded with some difficulty as I picked my way over another prickly, dry bush. The snow from the path had gone, leaving it dusty and dry. Here only bushes adorned with sharp red thorns lined the path. Trees were beginning to look leafier the further down we went, and I could hear the noise of water in the distance. Daya was ahead of me, and Zharabi flew overheard, listening intently. Keeping my eyes on Daya's constantly swaying tail, I remained silent as she continued her story.

"The spellbook was stolen from its maker by the Force, and has been kept in the shapeshifter's possession. The book, however, must return to another's hands before the sun and the moon unite. This is crucial, because at that moment whoever has the book will reign forever. If it is the Force, all light will be extinguished, and none of us will live. There are charts to determine when the uniting of the celestial bodies will take place, and a map that leads to the Ghost Monastery."

"How come the sorcerer can't get the spellbook?" I asked irritably as I eyed the seemingly endless number of prickly bushes that covered the path ahead.

"He has been gone for many centuries...Some even believe that he is nothing but a fable. We cannot rely on one who might be trapped by the Force's magic," replied Daya without looking back at me. Zharabi smiled down at me, clicking his beak to urge me along.

We walked until late afternoon. The sounds of a river were closer now, and the trees were like a lush green forest. I could also hear the sounds of humans in the distance. Voices, carts, and horses floated into my ears like a long-lost tune. The path we were following now was clearly used very often. Daya beckoned me off the path, and we trampled through the tall grass and into the trees.

There were no humans in the forest, presumably

because of the various wild animals we encountered. Large, poisonous cobras slithered out of our way as we strode through the forest, and black panthers stepped back respectfully, their yellow eyes glowing as they watched us pass silently. As the edge of the forest drew nearer, Daya stopped. Zharabi flew down to join us as Daya issued orders.

"You must steal a horse from one of the humans and ride it into the town. Once inside, search for the maps and star charts. They are most likely to be kept by the chief of the village."

"The chief! But that means he will have guards to protect them." I was dismayed.

"Did you think this was going to be easy?" Daya snapped irritably. I glared at her.

"No, but you don't have to make it sound impossible!"

Zharabi interjected quickly, "Stop fighting, both of you. There isn't time to argue. After our encounter with the Force by the bridge and ravine, it will have guessed that we will look for Rinzen."

"What does Rinzen mean?" I asked Zharabi.

"Holder of intellect. That is the name given to the maps and star charts, because whoever possesses them holds the knowledge to the location of the Ghost Monastery, and the time at which the sun and moon will unite."

I opened my mouth to speak when, on the other side of the trees that lined the forest, we heard voices. I instinctively dropped onto all fours, and crept quietly along the forest floor, Daya by my side. Her amber eyes narrowed as she looked through the trees.

"I will meet you outside the village," she whispered to me. I nodded, and continued to crawl to the edge of the forest, while Daya fell back. Zharabi flitted above my head, his wings moving noiselessly through the air.

Once we were at the edge of the forest, I clambered up a large neem tree, and hauled myself along the thickest branch, which dipped just above the golden stalks of the cornfield that lay beyond the forest. Pushing the olive green leaves aside, I peered down onto the cornfield, and watched cautiously as two men approached the shade of the neem tree in a cart.

They couldn't have been more different. The man driving the cart was large and comfortable looking, with skin that looked almost black, and hair nearly as dark. His eyes were a dull green and glittered in the late afternoon sunlight. He wore a cloth wrapped as pants around his legs, the dirt-streaked white folds hanging loosely around his legs. His belly protruded several inches, and around his neck was a golden chain.

The other man, who sat back with a whip in his hand to beat the horse if necessary, was bony and thin. His skin was a lighter, cocoa brown, and shone with sweat. He wore the same clothing as the fat man, but had a thinner gold chain around his neck. His black hair was plastered to his head, and he scanned the horizon with almond-shaped, dark brown eyes as the cart rolled along, its wheels squeaking sullenly with every turn.

My mouth went dry at the sight of these men, not with fear of my impending task, but at finally having found people who were similar to me in appearance.

"They look like me," I muttered to myself under my breath. Could my mother, Rani, have been from this village? I swallowed my excitement quickly, and focused on what I had to do. On the back of the wooden cart was a blanket that covered items of some sort. If I hid under the blanket, I could pass into the town unnoticed.

"Ready?" Zharabi's voice in my ear reassured me. I nodded, and climbed down from the neem tree. Hiding behind the knotted bark of the thick trunk, I waited until the cart had lazily rolled past the tree. Running low to the ground, I followed it for several moments before deftly leaping onto the back. As my weight shook the cart, I hastily threw the blanket over my body. I was surrounded by a medley of objects, from farming tools to pots and pans. Through the scratchy material, I could faintly see the rays of sun, bright through even my covering.

"What was that? The cart moved." One of the men spoke. I remained deathly still, my heart beating quickly.

"It was probably your imagination. Now shut up and whip the horse. I want to get back into town quickly." The fat man's voice was commanding, and soon a silence fell again. My muscles relaxed slightly, and I immediately wondered where Zharabi had gone. A hiss sounded behind me.

"Psst, Tien—it's me."

"Are you a snake?" I saw shiny black coils move next

to me. The tiny garden snake nodded its black eyes, its skin standing out from the silver pot it laid curled upon.

"You have to jump out the next time the cart stops. I'll signal you."

I nodded mutely, and waited. The cart rolled along the bumpy road, and the men struck up a conversation. Slowly, I shifted my body so that my face was at the edge of the cart. Lifting up the blanket, I peered out from under it.

Behind me lay large expanses of cornfields, the tall stalks waving peacefully and glowing in the sunlight. Behind the cornfields, growing farther in the distance, was the forest, a dark blemish on the otherwise civilized lands. To my right were more cornfields, and the out-skirts of the village. The houses were reminiscent of my old home with Wise Woman. Feeling a lump come into my throat, I looked away quickly, and saw a strange sight drawing close to the wooden cart.

Several large caravans rolled alongside the cart. On their chipped wooden sides were painted *Amir's Traveling Bazaar,* in curving red letters. Red flags that looked as though they had been made from cleaning rags were attached to poles, and carried by men and women dressed in black, their faces covered with cloth so that only their eyes could be seen. All of them rode silently on horses. I watched as they passed me. Suddenly, one rider galloped past the caravans. The rider wore a flowing black cloak, with a hood that was pulled over his head. Turning to look at me, the rider's strange golden eyes bore into my own. Frightened, I drew back. The rider hissed, "Tien Ming…" Then, without a backwards glance, he galloped onwards to the front of the line of caravans.

Pulling the blanket back over my head, I met the eyes of the black garden snake, and even though we did not speak, the two of us knew we were both wondering the same thing: how had the dark rider known my name?

Chapter Nine

Into the Village

After some time, I could hear more voices from all sides of the cart. Men and women of all ages called out in greeting to the two men driving the cart, who jovially returned the sentiments. I was, once again, reminded of my own village. The path was less bumpy now, and I ventured another glance from under the blanket.

Behind us stood two tall pillars that were evidently meant to be gates to the town. They were made of some kind of clay that glowed red in the light of the fading sun. Men stood beside every pillar, crossbows slung across their backs, and silver daggers held in their hands. The street that we traveled down was made of mud that had been pressed down by men's feet and horse's hooves so many times that it was plastered to the ground, hard and solid like dull red rock.

On either side of the street were colorful shops that sold everything from brass pots to gold jewelry. Women hurried from shop to shop, haggling cheerfully with every shopkeeper to get the best price. Everyone seemed to know one another somehow. Colorful clothing similar to mine was worn by the women, but their black hair was wavy, unlike my shiny, straight hair.

Suddenly, the cart rolled to a stop.

"Now!" Zharabi hissed in my ear. I threw the blanket off me, and jumped off the cart. Striding away quickly, I did not look back until I was a safe distance away. The two men were scratching their heads, wondering how the blanket had moved.

"Must have been the breeze," said the thin one. The fat man nodded in agreement, and they began to unload their assortment of materials into the doorway of a shop that bore a tattered sign that read *Weapons of All Kinds*.

I quickly turned and continued walking, making a mental note to get weapons at the first chance I had. Zharabi had changed form once again, and was now a tiny black butterfly resting almost unseen upon my shoulder.

"Just follow this road," the familiar voice whispered to me. "Don't talk to anyone. We need to find our way around first."

I nodded, and continued to make my way up the street. It wasn't easy; so many people were pushing to get to one shop or another that it took us several minutes to fight our way out of the main street, and onwards into the heart of the village.

The houses were growing steadily nicer now. The roofs were made of terracotta tiles instead of straw, and the structures had large wooden doors with complicated carvings etched on their blank faces. Servants dressed in bland clothing swept the stray dirt farther from houses with brooms that had uneven bristles.

As we continued down the single road, I realized that there were many other houses. Streets seemed to weave endlessly around me, like a maze. Turning, I could see the sun setting behind the mountains. The lumbering caravans were now at the entrance of the village. I felt my heart beat faster as I remembered the dark rider. Zharabi must have been thinking along the same lines, because he muttered, "We should hurry. It won't be safe at night."

I nodded, and began to jog along the lane. Torches were being lit now, because the sun was almost gone from the sky. At the end of the lane, we found nothing but a clay wall. I turned around, and prepared to go the other way, when Zharabi said quietly, "Wait. I think there is a house here."

"What? I can't see anything." I reached my hand out to touch the clay wall and prove my point, but I could not touch the wall. In fact, even as I tried to do so, I was thrown back twenty feet. After landing on the ground, hard, I scrambled up, and ran at the clay wall again. The same thing happened, but with more force. As I stood up, brushing dirt from my clothes, the black butterfly said in a hushed tone, "Look."

A shimmering wall had appeared before us, and something moved behind it. I took a step back, apprehensively, as the outline of a house began to appear. This one was bigger than all the rest; with three floors and guards around it, the structure seemed nothing short of a mansion to me.

"Why did it appear?" I asked Zharabi in a whisper. He flapped his miniscule wings in what I assumed was a shrug.

Striding up to the guards, I said, "Excuse me, but I was wondering who lived here."

The guards stayed still. I tried once more, in a louder voice.

"I am just a traveler, and I was hoping for some directions."

Still, a stony silence met my ears. Raising my voice to a shout I asked the first question again.

"EXCUSE ME, BUT I WAS WONDERI—"

"They can't hear you. No one can. I put a spell on the house to make it, and myself, unseen and unheard."

"Who said that?" I looked around wildly for the new voice. It was creaky and old, like the wheels of the cart I had ridden into town on.

At first, there was no response. Only the door of the house creaked open. Then a voice from the dark insides spoke.

"Enter."

I hesitated. There was a soft laugh, and the voice asked, "You are looking for Rinzen, are you not? If you are, then enter. If not, then leave, for I have no business with you."

Although I entered the house, I remained apprehensive, hoping that it was not a trap.

Chapter Ten

The Passing of Sangmu

The room inside the house was well furnished, with comfortable, multicolored chairs, and dark green rugs that covered most of the wooden floor. The chairs were centered on a wooden table with spindly legs. I stood awkwardly for a moment, looking around the room, until the voice sounded again.

"You might as well change to something more useful, Zharabi. The butterfly isn't doing anyone any good. I can barely see you."

The next moment, the air rippled and Zharabi had once more become a sleek black panther with dark, soulful eyes. Sitting next to me, he grinned, the perfect white teeth shining in the dull light from the torch.

"I was beginning to wonder whether you were as old as you looked."

The house laughed, shaking its foundations once more, and replied, "Not quite that old yet. I do not forget... Perhaps I should make this conversation a little easier?"

I blinked, and saw a tall figure appear from tendrils of smoke in the center of the room. It wore leathery pants that were tucked into brown boots. A loose white shirt was partially covered by a brown vest. The figure was draped in a hooded, dark green cloak that fell to its feet. The hood covered the face of the figure so well that I could not tell whether it was a man or woman. Sitting down on a chair, the figure motioned to another chair and said, "Please, sit. We have much to discuss, and little time."

I sat down on a chair with patches of red, blue, and green, and surveyed the figure curiously. A laugh came from the depths of the hood, like the tinkling of bells.

"I suppose you are wondering who I am. That question should be answered first. I presume that you, Zharabi, already have some idea?"

The black panther nodded, and replied quietly, "More of an idea than you can know, Sangmu."

The figure's voice suddenly became sharp and accusing. "You make it sound as though I have reduced myself to such a state, with this terrible disguise, and the cowardly hiding within the house! I did not want to come here, but I had no choice...I was not powerful enough. I have grown, if possible, even weaker since the day I fled from the mountains. I concealed myself, but my magic waned. As a result, a foolish man who believed he could tame magic caught me! He is the one who forced me to put a spell upon this house, and to guard Rinzen with my powers."

The figure hunched over for a moment, breathing heavily. Then, straightening up, it spoke softly, "My only chance of escape is for you to take Rinzen. I have only stayed here because I feared that someone else would capture Rinzen if I did not protect it. But if you take it, I will be able to free myself, and perhaps leave this world for another one…"

Pulling its hood back, the figure vanished into smoke. I jumped up, and looked around, but there was no sign of anyone else in the room. Then, from behind me, the voice of the figure sounded.

"I am here." A woman with dark skin and sleek, flowing black hair stood behind me. She might have been Indian but for her artfully slanted eyes that resembled those of the people from my old village. She looked neither old nor young, but seemed to glow with a purple light. She wore long, deep violet robes that billowed as she moved.

"Welcome back, Sangmu," said Zharabi. The woman turned and acknowledged him. Turning to me, she said, "Hello, Tien. My name is Sangmu. I am the witch who created the Golden Pass."

I eyed the woman's perfectly curved, oval face warily before speaking.

"I thought it was a wizard who created the Golden Pass."

My words seemed to upset Sangmu. She rolled her eyes, and said angrily, "Legend only glorifies men and those who are pure of race. Women of mixed race are least likely to command respect. As a child, I am sure you have come across criticism and taunts because of your mixed heritage?"

I nodded, and Sangmu made an angry gesture with her hands, the violet robes swaying like smoke around her.

"I too faced this, many centuries ago, when I was growing up. I realized, in time, that I possessed a power that others did not. I believe that I was the first of the human race to discover that there were other forces that could be manipulated and bent to one's will if you possessed such capabilities. I left the human world far behind me as I explored magic."

Sangmu laughed as she spoke, recalling more memories from her past.

"There were magical creatures, too, whom I befriended. I had become queen of another universe...I was able to cast away my past as a beggar." Tears rolled down the witch's face as she relived her former triumphs.

"But still, Tien, it was not enough for me to prophesize and see the future of the world. I wanted more, you see. I wanted those who had once seen me as worthless to see how powerful a mix of race can be. In other words, *I wanted to change the way other people viewed the world.*"

I felt sympathetic towards Sangmu, not because of her

plight, but because I felt the same way she did. If had been given the chance, I would have attempted to change the way others thought as well, just to be accepted.

Sangmu sank into a chair now, as though held down by iron weights. I followed suit, and sat close to her, watching as she continued to relive her horrible past.

"I was foolish. I see that now, looking back at what I did. Because, Tien, as breathtaking my powers were, as much as I could bend them to my will, I could not bend people to my will. It was, so to speak, the one power I lacked. But could it be done? I wondered if there was a dark way, perhaps, to bend men's weak minds into service."

Sighing, Sangmu looked at the ground. I said quietly, thinking of the evil Force, "There was a way. You created it, didn't you? The Force can bend people. That's why you left the mountains, and hid."

Sangmu's eyes were tired when she looked at me, and I saw how old she really was. The skin had become papery folds, and her hair was wispy and white. Then, in a flash, it was replaced by her magical appearance.

"While I created the Golden Pass, I also worked on another experiment, one that I hoped would be able to bend the minds of men. I worked tirelessly, putting into it what men crave: power, intellect, beauty…and magic! I hoped that this mixture would allow me to unite warring races under one banner, and make men see that mixed races are equal to pure races."

"But it went wrong," I said. "Didn't it?"

Sangmu nodded, and whispered so quietly that I had

to lean in to hear, "Oh yes. It went terribly wrong. For one who has power, beauty and magic that is not human... it is a dangerous mix. The Force was too powerful for me to handle from the beginning, because I had grown old. I am not afraid to admit this. In making the Golden Pass and creating the Force, my powers were weakened, and I could feel my strength ebbing. The Force wished to inhabit my body, and bend my mind. It said that together, we would rule the world."

"But I was smarter," Sangmu croaked. "The inhabitance of my body by the Force would have led to my death, and the destruction of many other innocent lives. With the belief that I would be saving others, I used the last of my strength to transport the Force to the Ghost Monastery."

"What is the Ghost Monastery?" I asked Sangmu.

"It is a breeding place for evil. The monks who lived there were actually evil spirits who captured souls and trapped them there for all eternity." As Sangmu spoke about the Ghost Monastery, I felt a chill in the air. Sangmu looked about wildly.

"They are coming." She began to mutter to herself. I looked at Zharabi, who simply shrugged.

"Who is coming? Why are they coming here?" Sangmu only shook her head, and refused to answer any of my questions.

"I must finish the story!" She was gasping for air now. Falling to her knees, she gripped the table, and looked into my eyes, determined to finish.

"I locked the Force in the monastery, and then I ran, Tien. I ran from magic, and from my false sense of power in the mountains. I came to this village, where I found Rinzen. I vowed to protect it with my life. The chief of the village trapped me on the Force's orders. The Force knows you...you...are...here. Take Rinzen! It is my soul...Rinzen is my soul...You must find a safe place to read it, where others cannot see."

Grabbing my hand, Sangmu said in an uncharacteristically harsh voice, "Forgive me. I could have changed your fate, but I did not....because I wanted to see another powerful sorceress rise like myself. Forgive me..."

"I forgive you! But how did you know my name?" I finally voiced the question that had been nagging at the back of my mind. Sangmu only smiled at me, her beautiful features more pronounced than ever. Her grip loosened upon my hand, and there was a loud bang. Her body was gone, lost in the shower of violet sparks that had suddenly sprung from the ground. They rocketed into the air, and bounced off the walls of the room, finally coming together in the center and exploding with several loud crashes. I was thrown against the wall, and blinded by the burst of light. When it had finally faded, there was no sign of Sangmu.

"Where did she go?" I asked Zharabi, as he paced the room, still a black panther.

"She has...passed on." He did not look sad as he said this.

"You mean...she died?"

Zharabi laughed at the incredulous look on my face. "Sangmu wanted to pass on. Her name means 'kind hearted one,' you know…I think she was just that, until the very end."

"Look!" I pointed to the center of the room, where a tall flower had sprung up. It had a slender but firm green shoot with violet, heart-shaped petals at the end. There were several of these, clustered together. Bending down, I touched a petal. It was as soft as velvet. Glimmering violet sparks flew off the petal as I touched it a second time. "What is it?" I breathed, amazed.

"It is Sangmu's heart," replied Zharabi. He was next to me now, bending low over the flower, his triangular nose sniffing gently. His eyes filled with tears.

"I-I can remember!" His voice was strangely jubilant. Then, after a moment, he looked at me with a strange mixture of pity and fear upon his face.

I was about to ask Zharabi what he remembered when there was a knock at the door. At once, the candles that had dimly lit the room went out, leaving only Rinzen, bathed in a small circle of violet light. Zharabi and I hurried to the corner of the room, and leapt behind a chair.

The door creaked open; in the shaft of dim evening light spilling through the small opening, I could see the dark rider outlined clearly. The rider shut the door behind them, and called out in a deep, male voice, "Sangmu, where are you?"

It was then that his eyes fell upon the beautiful flower. I heard a sharp intake of breath, and saw a large hand dip down to uproot the flower. As his fingers closed around it, there was another bang, and the room was filled with light. Violet flames issued from the tip of the flower, scorching the man. He roared with pain, and stumbled back, his hood falling to reveal his face.

His curly black hair was tousled, and complemented his deep green eyes. Every feature upon his face was so flawless that he appeared almost inhuman. I knew, in the instant the hood fell back from this man's face, that I must grab Rinzen and run away. I stood up from behind the chair, and sprinted toward the inferno of violet flames that were now as high as the roof. Yanking Rinzen unceremoniously from the floor, I turned to meet the glowing green eyes. The man drew his sword, and swung at me. I jumped, and the low swing of the dagger missed my feet by mere inches.

From my right, a black ball of fur leapt at the man, knocking the sword out of his hands. Diving, I snatched the blade up, and held it to the man's throat. Zharabi held him against the wall, snarling angrily. I put the blade against the man's throat, still clutching Rinzen with my right hand.

"Who are you? What do you want?" My voice was demanding and loud, a new tone I had never used before.

"My-my name is Amir. I want the flower!"

"Do you know what this is?" The man cowered with fear as I pressed the dagger closely against his throat.

"N-no, I don't—I swear!" He added the last part hastily after Zharabi pushed him harder against the wall with a menacing growl.

"Then who sent you?" Amir went pale with fright as Zharabi spoke.

"I live here!" Amir spoke indignantly. "That traveling bazaar was with me to get passage into the city. There was a boy...h-he told me to say your name..." Amir pointed a shaking finger at Tien, "to see if you would respond! And you did. He told me that he would take my entire village if I did not let his bazaar in, which was named after me. He's...he's coming after nightfall..." Amir trailed off, still shaking with fear.

Continuing to hold the blade to Amir's throat, I flung the door open. The cool night air rushed in, and I saw that the moon was rising. Was it my imagination, or were the black shadows of the men who had killed Wise Woman already creeping over the houses towards me?

"We have to get out of here," I said to Zharabi. "The moon is rising...They'll be here soon."

"What about him?" Zharabi jerked his head towards Amir. I shrugged.

"I don't care. What do you want to do with him?"

Zharabi growled, and raised a paw to strike Amir to the ground. He pleaded desperately, "Please! Don't hurt me...all I want is my life. I'll run away, so that those men won't find me." He was blubbering like a child now. I chanced another look out the door. There was no mistaking it now; men were definitely climbing over the houses, running down the path like swarming ants.

"We have to go!" Zharabi nodded. Leaving Amir slouched in the doorframe gasping for air, Zharabi and I ran out the door, and turned right, heading towards the edge of the village. My heart beat fast with fear as I held my new sword tightly in one hand, and clutched the strange flower Rinzen in my other.

Chapter Eleven

Chased by Shadows

"We're never going to make it!" I cried to Zharabi as we skidded down yet another tiny alley. We had long since left Amir and his house behind; our only guide was Rinzen, glowing brighter than ever.

"Faster!" Zharabi was already at the end of the street, his long black tail twitching impatiently. I ran toward him as fast as I could, feeling my lungs burn with the effort. I turned, and saw the black shadows creeping over houses, cloaking the moon's bright glow with their darkness. Then, a familiar voice called out my name.

"Tien! You can't run forever..." I stood still for a moment, the black shadow looming over me, as I tried to remember where I had heard the voice before. The shadowy figures crept closer to me now, their black cloaks sweeping through the night air like wings. The leader snarled, "Give me Rinzen."

"You!" I gasped, and stumbled back. The leader laughed.

"It's been awhile since I saw you…It is a pity about Wise Woman, isn't it?" His sneering tone filled me with a fury that I had never felt before. As I felt the blood pounding in my head, a voice spoke to me, the voice of Sangmu. *Swing down upon his right arm.* I glanced at Rinzen, and realized that it had been the flower, directing me. Lunging at him, I swung my sword at his right arm. A cry of pain told me I had made my mark. The boy was now crouched on the ground, clutching his arm, and panting. Malicious eyes glittered at me through the eyeholes cut in the black cloth tied around his forehead and eyes.

"You'll regret that." He stood, and wiped his bloody right arm on his shirt. Raising his hand, he murmured words under his breath. To my horror, I saw a small ball of silver light crackling in his palm. He pushed his palm forward, and the electricity shot towards me. I ducked and rolled across the muddy, gravelly earth just in time. I heard the soft whoosh of the silver electricity before it hit the ground. There was a muffled explosion, and I shielded my eyes from the mud. Peering between my fingers, I saw a crater in the ground where I had been standing only moments before. Grabbing my sword, I jumped up, and sprinted down the alley, never looking back.

"GET HER!" shrieked the boy. I ran even faster, my arm weighed down by the heavy sword and Rinzen. Where was Zharabi? I looked around at the end of the road, but there was no sign of him. I could feel the cold, bitter wind that accompanied the Force beginning to blow through the otherwise still night. Holding Rinzen up, I said, more to myself than the flower, "Come on, come on…Can you hear me?" It sounded stupid as soon as I had said it. Still, I tried again.

"Come on, Rinzen, help me! Give me something more than light!" For a moment, the flower glowed brighter than ever. Behind me, the wind slowed, and I could sense the shadows falling back from the light. Keeping my eyes focused on the dark alleyway ahead of me, I shouted to Rinzen, "Help me find a way out of this!"

The flower shot violet flames into the air once more, but to my surprise, I was not burned by them. Like water from a fountain, the flames gracefully arced through the air, and then fell to the ground, illuminating the path for me.

"Thank you," I said gratefully to the flower. The shadows were on my heels now; I could hear the whispery voices of the men, as they urged me to give them Rinzen. I felt myself almost giving in to their gentle pleas, but then Sangmu's words echoed in my head: *I wondered if there was a dark way, perhaps, to bend man's weak mind into service.*

"No!" I realized that I was speaking aloud, but did not care. I would not allow the Force to bend my mind, not after it had taken Wise Woman from me. I could see the edge of the village now; the sound of the rushing river was filling my ears. Yet, with every step I took, my lungs burned and my legs trembled as though they could carry my weight no longer. I stumbled, and fell, face first, onto the ground. Rinzen tumbled out of my hand, and the violet flames vanished. I could see the flower glowing faintly still, only a few feet away.

But now the shadows swarmed all around me, and I was covered in darkness. I could no longer see Rinzen, or any other form of light. The moon became a dark, sinister orb, and I heard the whispers of the men once more, in my ears, telling me that I would die now. I felt my body grow weak as I looked into the eyes of the leader. But then I remembered Wise Woman, and I saw the torches lighting her body once more. I felt bitter and angry.

As the wind blew around me, I shouted at it, "I didn't do anything! I didn't do anything wrong, and you still took my mother and father. Why?" I stood up, wanting an answer. There was no reply; the wind simply continued to blow, biting at my arms and face like a wild animal.

"Why can't you answer me?" I was shrieking in order to be heard now. The men were nothing but blurred shapes and mere outlines in the wind. I felt as though I was part of a distorted painting, screaming at the figures inside it, even though I knew they could—or would— not hear me.

Despair swept over me, and I felt myself beginning to succumb to the Force's power, when a whispery voice crept through my head. Sangmu spoke to me once more. *Your sword, Tien. Slash the wind with it! It is the only way to escape.*

Obeying the voice, I bent down, picked up the sword, and swung it through the wind. There was a howl from beyond the swirling vortex that I was trapped in.

"Let me out!" I was angry now. Swinging again, I heard the wind shriek, but it became slower. I could see Rinzen again, glowing in the darkness of the alley. The men were now circling me again, the whispers were rising...and then suddenly, out of the darkness hurtled a golden blur. My heart lifted when I heard Daya roar. The shadows stepped back.

"Golden snow leopard...go, back to the mountains. You do not mix with humans." The leader stepped forward once more as he spoke. I did not wait for what Daya had to say; snatching Rinzen up, I yelled, "Daya, I have it. Run!"

But she did not run. Standing her ground, Daya said calmly, "Those rules no longer exist. You changed the mountains, so now I have changed my loyalties. I will not help those who desire the spellbook for their own personal gain."

Out of the shadows came a sleek black panther. Zharabi stood next to Daya, shielding me from the dark shadows. I backed slowly towards the edge of the village. Then, breaking into a run, I sprinted across the cornfields, holding Rinzen above my head triumphantly. Behind me, the soft, padded steps of the leopard and the panther sounded upon the dirt, closely followed by the whispering of the men. Soon, Zharabi and Daya were on either side of me, urging me on.

"There is a cliff, Tien—we have to jump, there's no other way..." Daya was cut off by Zharabi, who said, "Jump? We'll fall into the river, which leads to the dark side of the mountain!"

"If we don't jump, they will take us there anyway!" roared Daya angrily.

As she sped up, vanishing at the end of the cornfield, the familiar, deep smell of water and dirt reached my nose. Feeling as though my legs would rip apart with the effort, I burst out from between the tall stalks of corn. By the light of Rinzen, I could see Daya standing at the edge of the land, looking down. Then, with a graceful leap, she pitched over the edge and out of sight.

As Zharabi and I hurried to the edge of the cliff, shadows began to engulf us again. Not willing to be deterred, I raised Rinzen. Violet flames erupted from the flower's center once more, throwing back the shadows. Zharabi wasted no time in following Daya into the river.

For a moment that seemed to stretch forever, I stood at the edge of the cliff, looking down at the pounding waves of the river that glistened in the moonlight. Turning to look back, my eyes met those of the leader who sneered, "You're trapped now."

Shaking my head, I watched as the shadows drew closer to me. Then, with a smile upon my face, I jumped off the cliff, and into the rushing river below, leaving the whispers of the dark shadows and the Force behind.

Chapter Twelve

Reading Rinzen

The water felt like an icy hand from the moment I touched it. As I sank into the murky, unclear river, I felt Rinzen in one numb hand, and my sword in the other. Gripping them tightly, I saw a stray log floating to my left. Raising my sword from the water, I plunged it into the ancient bark of the log, and hoisted myself into a sitting position, holding my sword for support.

The moon was shining brighter than ever, illuminating the murky water of the river. Spitting out muddy water, I wiped my mouth, and lay down on the log, feeling cold and miserable. Daya and Zharabi were nowhere to be seen, the shadows were still at large, and all I had to show for my battle was a flower and a sword.

I lay Rinzen down carefully on the log, and spoke to it.

"So what else can you do, besides giving off flames and light?"

As if to respond to me, the flower let off deep purple flames that arced above my head. I turned around, and saw a black dolphin leap into the air. It waved a fin at me in greeting before diving back under the water.

"Zharabi!"

The dolphin popped its smooth head up by the log, and said, "I'm glad to see you, but I don't know where Daya is. We should stay on the river, though. This will lead us to the next area where our passage into the mountains will not be noticed. And…" the dolphin inclined its head towards the glowing flower, "a place where we can read Rinzen."

"You have to be in a special place to read it?"

The dolphin shook its head, bobbing up and down in the water.

"No, just somewhere that is hidden from others."

"I wonder where Daya is…" I scanned the murky water for any sign of her head, but saw none.

"She might be further ahead, you know. She jumped off before we did, and the river is moving pretty fast," said Zharabi reassuringly. "Stay here while I search for her."

As the dolphin ducked under the water and vanished in the murk, I picked up Rinzen again, feeling the velvet petals gently. I held it above the water, looking for any sign of Daya, but there was none.

I continued to drift down the river for the rest of the night alone, searching the empty waters for Daya. More villages lined the river, but all were deserted, and seemed ghostly by the light of the moon. Occasionally, in the distance, I saw the black head of a dolphin in the water, but then it would vanish once more. The water was soon no longer murky, and became so clear that I could see to the surprisingly deep bottom of the river. It was sandy, littered with various rocks of all shapes and sizes.

The sun rose slowly over the mountains that were to my left. The river had grown wide and shallow now, and was flowing slowly due to the pebbles that covered its bed. The log I was crouched upon had stopped moving. With Rinzen and my sword still clutched in my hands, I jumped off the log, and looked around.

I was on a bank of medium-sized rocks that had been rubbed smooth and flat by the river's constant rush of water. To my left loomed the Himalayas, the snow on their peaks glistening in the early morning sunlight.

"Tien! Over here!"

I turned to see a wet black owl shaking out its feathers while it waited for me. Crossing the remainder of the river, I asked Zharabi, "So no sign of Daya?"

The owl shook its head. "No. She might have gone back on her own...I was surprised she even helped us last night."

I nodded, but felt a sinking feeling in my stomach. So Daya, just like the countless others in my village, had turned on me.

Zharabi must have noticed the dismayed look on my face, because he said gently, "Sangmu was right, Tien. You cannot change others...only yourself." There was a pause, and I nodded. Zharabi seemed convinced that I was feeling better, because he said, "Come on, we'd better try to read Rinzen."

I followed him as we walked alongside the rocky slope of the mountains. Grass grew at our feet, mixed in with bits and pieces of rock that had undoubtedly come from the mountains. The river was on our left, winding close to the narrow path we took. Across the stream I could see people waking in the villages, and coming down to the river to wash their clothes. A small part of me wished that I could be part of one of those villages, and have a real family.

Zharabi's whispered tones brought me back to the present, "Here! This looks good."

We had reached a small crevice in the endless rock. Zharabi flitted inside, and I bent down low to follow him.

Once my eyes had adjusted to the light, I was able to see a medium-sized cave, with smooth, curving walls. One large stone protruded from one wall in the cave, similar to a long bench. Curled up on it, in a ball, was a shivering golden leopard.

"Daya?" Zharabi sounded surprised.

She lifted her head from the rock momentarily.

"I was wondering when you would get here!" She spoke irritably.

"We thought you...left." I felt my heart surge with joy

at the thought that Daya had not gone after all. Despite her surly attitude, I couldn't help but feel warmly towards the golden snow leopard.

"Why would I leave?" Daya looked from me to Zharabi. When neither of us replied, she lay her head back down on the stone, and closed her large, round, amber eyes.

"So are you going to read Rinzen?" She spoke between shivers. I noted that her fur was still soaked from the river.

"Where were you in the river?"

At first, Daya ignored Zharabi's question, but as the silence deepened, she raised her head once more to speak.

"I had some difficulties swimming. I finally managed to climb out a few minutes ago, in the shallower part of the river. That's why I'm still wet. This cave was the only sheltered place to go on this side of the mountain, and I didn't want to sit out alone in the sun. Now are you going to read Rinzen or not?"

I nodded, and sat in the center of the cave, making a mental note that Daya did not like to be seen as weak. Placing Rinzen on the floor, I was momentarily blinded as it glowed with a strange white light. As the light died away, I heard Daya mutter her thanks. Turning around, I saw that she was no longer wet. As a matter of fact, neither were Zharabi or I.

I turned back to the flower, and watched as it sat on the gray floor of the cave, glowing with the same violet light.

"Listen…if you don't mind, I'd like to see the star charts and maps?" I was unsure of how to address the flower. Daya and Zharabi remained still behind me. Rinzen wriggled once, twice, and then a third time before spouting a small funnel of sunshine-yellow liquid from its center. The liquid arced through the air and splattered against the stretch of gray wall opposite me. The splatter then began to flatten, and spread across the wall, the thin strands reminding me of a spiderweb. As the yellow covered the wall, it began to sprout strange shapes that protruded off the wall a few inches, like ugly boils. Then the colors began to change, displaying everything from a lush green to an ink black. I stood up, amazed, as a life size map of the Himalayan Mountains sprang up before my eyes.

"Wow! Amazing…" I trailed off as I ventured closer to the map. Putting my finger on what looked like the Golden Pass, I followed the trail highlighted in violet ink, which led to the ravine that we had crossed, that the map called Perilous Ravine. From there, the violet trail went upwards, higher into the mountains, passing even the Bamboo Grove, which I noticed seemed to be at the center of the map. I walked up and down the wall, studying the various places upon the map.

"Oh look, they have a Dragon Pass too! I didn't think dragons actually existed…"

"They do," said Daya grimly. "We used to have land disputes with them, but I doubt any exist now. The Force has caused most magical animals to become extinct or very rare, because they cannot survive the dark shadows it casts over the mountains. It is like a poison to us."

I was barely listening to Daya; I had found another point of interest. "Sacred Forest. I wonder what lives in there?"

"Many things, actually. Sangmu herself used to reside there, before she was driven from the mountains."

Daya nodded, and I suddenly wondered why she hadn't asked how we had gotten Rinzen, so I asked her. Daya shrugged without looking at me. "You met her. Sangmu, I mean. She passed on, didn't she?"

"How did you know she passed on? And how did you know she was a girl? Sangmu told us that."

"You are not the only one who has spoken with Sangmu. Every magical creature knew her very well. She regarded us as her children. She thought of the Force as her child too, you know. That's why she could not destroy it at the beginning. She always said she was too weak... but I think that had she tried, the Force could have been vanquished. But she was well named, Sangmu. Kind-hearted and gentle."

Zharabi said pityingly, "She was insane in the end, Daya. You would not have recognized her. I think the death of magical creatures hurt her."

Daya simply said, "Then I am glad that I was not there to witness it."

There was silence after that, while each of us looked at the map. I followed one line of violet ink past the Dragon Pass, through the Steps of Death, and finally to the Ghost

Monastery, where a human skull leered unpleasantly at me. I pulled my hand away from the map quickly.

"That's it," said Daya quietly. "We must pass the Steps of Death..." she shuddered.

"What's wrong with the Steps?" I asked.

"No human has passed through them alive," she said quietly. "They capture lives."

An uncomfortable silence followed Daya's dire words.

Zharabi broke it, asking, "Is there another way? I would rather we didn't go through the Dragon Pass." He looked both dismayed and worried when Daya shook her head.

"It's the quickest way from this side of the mountain. Now, what about the star charts? Those are going to be harder to read."

I nodded, and reluctantly asked the flower, "May we see the star charts please?"

The flower twitched again, and the map vanished in one blink. In its place was squirted midnight blue ink, and I soon found myself looking at a display of the solar system, the planets floating a few inches from the wall.

Daya was studying the map intently. She asked Zharabi, "Do you see the sun?"

He nodded, and indicated the yellow-orange orb. Daya lifted a paw and pointed to the moon, which was silvery and luminous.

"Do you think I could ask Rinzen to calculate it?" I felt stupid asking the question, but Zharabi shrugged his wings in assent.

"It's worth a try."

Turning to the flower, I said tentatively, "Do you think you could calculate the time until the sun and the moon unite?"

Rinzen glowed brightly, and after a moment, on the far corner of the map, smooth, curving writing in white ink appeared. Zharabi flew up to the lettering, and read, "Two months, fifteen days, forty-two hours, and thirty-seven minutes."

"Two months is a long time!" I felt relief rush through me. Daya and Zharabi laughed.

"Two months," began Daya, "is not nearly enough time. When you have lived for centuries, two months is only a minute in time."

"We need to leave now." Zharabi sounded rushed.

"What about Rinzen?"

"We have to destroy it." Daya spoke grimly. "Sangmu will not have passed on completely until the flower is destroyed."

I suddenly understood why the flower had been able to guide me in using a sword; Sangmu was trying to teach me.

"We can't destroy Sangmu's heart. She helped me fight the shadows!" I was angry at Daya for even suggesting such a thing. She opened her mouth to retort, but Zharabi said quickly, "Do not fight now; we have very little time. Bring the flower with you, Tien. Come on!"

Zharabi slipped out of the cave, and Daya followed him. Grabbing Rinzen, I exited the cave, looking back only once at the fading images on the wall.

Chapter Thirteen

Encountering the Dragon King

We hurried across the grassy field, heading back upstream. Zharabi flew low to the ground, forcing me to run doubled over. Daya, too, crouched as she walked, for fear of being seen. I sensed the shadows that had previously pursued us, but when I turned to look, there was no such darkness in sight.

The sun's rays began to beat down upon us until we had reached the shade of the mountains. I could see a narrow path, now overgrown by weeds, leading into the craggy peaks. I remembered the last time I had run up a similar mountain path, and wondered if I would find yet another astonishing creature on this trail.

"Follow me, and be quiet," muttered Zharabi. He had changed back into a black panther. Feeling uneasy, I followed him, and Daya brought up the rear, her tail twitching nervously.

We climbed slowly up the old path. Flanking us on ether side like gray giants were the sloping sides of the mountains. Dark clouds that looked heavy with rain covered the sun, and my high spirits were soon gone.

The trail widened after some time, and we found ourselves looking at a large expanse of gravel-covered ground, with caves that seemed to have been carved from within the mountains. The empty, dark holes gaped at us, making me shiver.

"This is Dragon Pass," whispered Daya. Her voice echoed up and down the wide ravine, but there was no other sound.

As we wove our way through the pass, I noticed that whatever greenery had been flourishing before was now gone. Limp weeds lined either side of the path, but everything else seemed to have been burned out of the way. The mountainsides here were peppered with black burn marks that I presumed had come from dragons battling over the years.

Suddenly, a loud roar sounded throughout the pass. I jumped, startled, and held the sword I had stolen from Amir at the ready. Zharabi and Daya looked around, but there was no one else in sight.

"What was that?" I asked in hushed tones.

"A dragon," said Zharabi.

I looked at him, open-mouthed, but he had begun to walk faster.

"We need to get out of here. Come on!"

He increased his loping strides, but I did not follow him. A cave far up on the mountain had caught my eye. From deep within it, I saw a red glimmer, moving in and out of sight slowly.

"It's a dragon," I whispered, amazed. Ignoring Daya and Zharabi's protests, I began to climb up the mountainside, using the large rocks as my footholds. I passed several empty caves with no sign of their past inhabitants. When I finally climbed up to the cave where I had seen the red glimmer, I found that I was able to see past Dragon Pass, and further into the dark side of the mountains. Turning, I looked into the dark mouth of the cave, and saw two large, cat-like green eyes looking back at me.

"Are you a dragon?" As I spoke, I heard Daya and Zharabi shift nervously behind me.

The eyes moved closer to me, and the dragon came out of the darkness of the cave. I was so shocked that I did not think to move away, or to draw my sword to protect myself. I simply stood and watched, my hands hanging limply at my sides, as a beast the length and width of four sailboats rumbled out of its cave.

The dragon's nose was long, and fairly wide, with two large nostrils at the end. Textured spikes lined its spine, beginning from the back of its head, and continuing until the tip of the tail. It had leathery wings that lay folded against its sides. The short, rather stout legs looked strong, and each foot had four sharp black talons at the end that reminded me of fingers.

The dragon did not speak when it saw us, but only bent its long neck to sniff at me. The red scales glimmered and winked like gems and stars. Drawing back, the dragon said in a surprisingly human voice, "So Sangmu has passed on."

I nodded, registering that the voice of the dragon was that of a young male.

"Hmph. Why are you here then? I thought everyone had given up hope." The dragon curled its tail closer to its body, and I saw a black mark that had taken away the shine and color from the red scales. Noticing my gaze, the dragon said sadly, "The result of the final battle that took my people. Luckily, I was able to hide..." The dragon stopped talking, and a lone tear rolled from its emerald-like eyes and fell to the ground.

Gathering up my courage, I stepped forward, and introduced myself.

"My name is Tien Ming."

The dragon studied me carefully, and I returned the intense gaze. After a long silence, the dragon replied, "My name is Struptha. I was once a great dragon, a king of my people...but now, my time is over. I have little hope these days...and now Sangmu is gone. You should return home, Tien Ming. There is nothing for you here, only an evil Force that will destroy us all."

Struptha turned to re-enter his cave. I said after him, "I have no home. I don't even have a family."

Struptha craned his long neck to look at me. He replied, "I am not much better off than you. I am compelled to hide in my cave in order to avoid the power of the Force. It is still searching, you know. Every day, it comes to look for any remaining traces of magic. My scales grow weary of waiting, but there is no way to shorten my life."

"I know how you feel." It was Daya who spoke. She stepped forward. Struptha looked surprised.

"A golden snow leopard? I thought you had all gone. My respects, princess."

He bowed his head to Daya. She bowed to him in return.

"The same to you, King of Dragons."

Struptha laughed bitterly. "I am no king. Look at my kingdom! I have no land, no subjects...I am alone. The Force took everything from me."

"Princess?" I looked at Daya, but she did not answer me. Instead she spoke to Struptha.

"Come with us to avenge the Force! If we gather the remaining creatures, perhaps we can vanquish the evil."

The dragon shook his head. "It is impossible."

Zharabi finally spoke. "It is not impossible. We are only two months away from the time that the sun and the moon will unite!"

"But it will take longer than that to get the spellbook! You do not even know where it is. And then, when darkness cloaks the land, there will be chaos." Struptha raised a talon, and pointed it to the wall.

Images appeared at once, of men, women, and children lying dead upon the ground. Others were screaming, and running from their burning homes, chased by the shadows of the Force.

These images were replaced by others. Unicorns galloped through the mountains, but were struck down as the sun slowly began to fade. The bodies of dragons fell from the sky, thudding against the ground heavily. And finally, the moon rose high in the sky, victorious...but then the moon turned into the shimmering ball that was the Force.

Struptha lowered his talon. "That is the fate that awaits this world when the spellbook is captured by the Force."

"Then why do you not want to help us?" I could not help but sound accusatory. "You have such knowledge of what will happen, yet you seem content to watch the world shatter around you!"

Struptha turned his large eyes upon me, but I was not afraid. After a moment, he lowered his head sadly.

"I will not live much longer, and the age of magic is ending. There is no use in my fighting a battle that has already been lost."

"The battle isn't lost," I said quietly. "It has barely begun. Join us, and fight the Force. Think of your people that were killed by the Force's magic. Your kind will be forgotten if you do not make them memorable."

Struptha smiled at me, his sharp white teeth contrasting with his large pink tongue.

"What makes you think that you will have a chance

in defeating the Force? You are only a child, with two companions."

"I don't think that I have a great chance," I replied. "But I have to try."

My words seemed to displease Struptha, who gave an impatient sigh, black smoke unfurling from his nostrils as he exhaled.

"Then good luck to you, foolish child."

There was a long pause, during which I looked at Struptha. Finally, he bent down so that his nose was mere inches from my face.

"I am afraid that I do not have enough strength to journey with you. But…your heart is pure, and you have determination I have not seen in man for many years. If there is a final battle, I will come to your aid. Here."

Tilting his head away from me, Struptha blew green flames onto the rock before us. As they died out, a small shell strung on a simple gold chain appeared upon the rock, glimmering.

"If you blow into this shell, it will call to the remaining magical creatures. They will come, for the final battle…if there are any left."

"Thank you." I took the shell, and placed it upon my neck.

Struptha looked at me, and said, "There is just one more thing I wish you to do for me. In the Ghost Monastery, there is a room where the Force has kept dragon eggs, unicorn foals, golden snow leopard cubs, and other children of the ancient creatures hidden. Free them, Tien. Please…that is my only wish."

I gulped and nodded, looking into the dragon's eyes. "I promise."

"Thank you." Struptha slowly returned to his cave. We watched until the darkness swallowed him. Then, with more grim determination than ever, Daya, Zharabi, and I approached the Steps of Death, wondering what we would find next.

Chapter Fourteen

The Ruler of the Ghost Monastery

"I don't understand it. How did this happen?"

The young man paced the large room angrily. His brown hair was tugged at in fury and frustration, and his eyes glowed a silvery white.

"Why do you worry so?" A whispery voice sounded from behind the young man. He whipped around quickly, and fell to his knees instantly, the cold ground pressing into his forehead as he prostrated himself in front of his master.

The woman looked down at him, contempt and revulsion etched upon her beautiful features. Her black hair flowed smoothly down her back, a thick curtain that blended with the man's tunic, pants and boots she wore.

The boy slowly looked up, as though he dared not glance at the creature in front of him. The woman let out a mirthless laugh at his fear, and turned on her heel, striding toward a golden throne in the center of the room.

"You believe I worry too much?" The boy was panting as he spoke, and beads of sweat appeared at his temple.

"How can you even say that? I failed twice—TWICE now. She's only a child. I don't understand it…"

The woman raised her eyebrows at the boy, and he fell silent almost immediately.

"She's more than a child. Look at her." The woman pointed to the blank castle wall, and an image of Tien appeared.

The boy stared at it with distaste, and then snapped, "This wasn't supposed to happen. I was supposed to be the next powerful sorcerer. You told me I would be!" He pointed a finger accusingly at the woman, who replied in a bored tone, "You will be the most powerful sorcerer. Once Tien is out of the way, everything will be yours to take."

"Then why couldn't we kill her when she was a child, after forcing the password out of her?" The boy was pacing once more. The woman said with a bite of impatience in her voice, "Because we must first extend her an offer of friendship!"

The boy rolled his eyes. "We should have shackled her the way we shackled Sangmu—they are all the same, too weak to resist your powers."

The woman snorted. "Sangmu was child's play. She was weak and old, and her bond to me made her easy prey. Tien is bound to no one. I cannot bend her mind to my will as easily."

"What do you mean?" For the first time, the boy raised his voice. The woman turned to him, her emotionless eyes like pools of silver liquid.

"She will not obey me. It is because she is bound to no one. Love exerts no power over her as it does the other weak humans in the world."

"Why?" The boy looked intrigued.

"She has been taught not to love," said the woman quietly. "When she was young, Tien was despised by others...She never learned to love."

"I don't think so...I think she likes that shapeshifter." The boy was slouching against the stone wall, his face screwed up with concentration while he pondered the thought.

"Likes? You mean....loves?" A hungry look appeared in the woman's silver eyes. Leaning back on the chair she lounged upon, the woman asked the boy, "That is the one we spoke with before, is it not?"

The boy was rubbing his hands together eagerly, silver sparks flying between them like fire. "Oh yes...that is Zharabi. He was once the fool alchemist's pet; or more astutely, his magical *protector*. And if I am not mistaken, once we force him to take human form, affection will spring between them."

The woman threw her head back and laughed a chilling, cruel laugh. "Brilliant. If your theory works, then we will eventually have our chance to kill Tien, and ensnare

Zharabi in a powerful trap...I assume he knows the dangers of this." The woman looked disappointed for a moment, but her face brightened when the boy said impatiently, "Of course he knows, but I'm not sure if he remembers...We made that bargain to save his master's life years ago. He may have forgotten by now."

The woman smirked in a self-satisfied manner, her slim, dark hands curled around the handles of the throne. She stood, and said to the boy, "I hope you will carry this plan out without fail."

The boy crossed his arms and smiled. "Of course, Master...after all, I am the Ruler of the Ghost Monastery." His tone held a pride and confidence that displeased the woman. Anger licked at her insides like a burning fire.

"That, you most certainly are," she said calmly, "But remember...I am your master." A cruel, cold look crossed her face, and the boy bowed almost instantly.

"Of course, of course...you, Master, are above everyone." The boy knelt at the foot of the chair. The woman regarded him contemptuously as he touched his head to the tips of her black boots, trembling with fear. Without another word, the woman stepped over the boy as though he were nothing more than an ant, and twirled gracefully. The boy whipped around, but she had already melted into the shadows of the darkness, the glimmer of her silver eyes fading last. With a sigh, the boy took her place in the chair, rubbing his hands together and chuckling softly to himself while he waited alone in the ever-deepening darkness.

Chapter Fifteen

The Steps of Death

"Well, it doesn't look too bad," I said, attempting to be optimistic. The Steps of Death loomed in front of us, weaving endlessly up the mountain. Rinzen was held in my left hand, and my sword in my right. I could feel the pulsing of the flower as it continued to glow a shocking violet. I felt my heart lift as the flower grew warm in my hand.

"This is going to take us until nightfall," Zharabi said. He transformed into a small butterfly once more, and settled on my shoulder. Daya led the way, not speaking, but looking more serious than I had ever seen her. I wondered if the encounter with Struptha had shaken her; she seemed to have fallen silent after we had left him behind. But why had he addressed her as princess? It suddenly occurred to me that Daya, Struptha, and other magical creatures that were still resisting the Force's power might have been able to do so for such a long period of time because they were the leaders of their own kind.

"Did royalty have any special powers?" I waited while the small butterfly considered what I had said.

"It depends. Traditionally, dragons blessed their leaders with more powers so that when the time came, the strongest dragon would lead them into battle. I don't know if other animals did this, but I can tell you that most of the remaining creatures have only survived so far out of pure luck."

We were halfway up the stairs now, and the sun was setting behind the mountains. A light drizzle had begun to fall, and darker clouds approached the Steps of Death, suggesting a storm was imminent.

"None of the creatures have survived because of pure luck," snapped Daya. She turned to face us, her impressive form exuding a light of its own in the dying sun.

"I wasn't suggesting you personally did." Zharabi seemed unwilling to fight with Daya. She glowered at him for a moment, and it was only after I passed her on the steps that she continued to follow us.

I noticed that the higher we climbed the more bones littered the steps. At first, the old, grayish stone only had green, bristly moss growing upon it, but as we continued to ascend, I saw bones of all shapes and sizes. Some of them looked human, but I simply averted my eyes, and focused on the top of the stairs, which was now in sight. I could see two pillars made of white marble on either side of the staircase.

I noticed, with a jolt, that the sky had grown ominously dark, and that the sun's rays were no longer seen in this area. When I had clambered over the last few stairs, panting slightly, I looked closely at the white pillars.

The marble had undoubtedly been well taken care of at one point; now, however, either moss or vines covered whatever splendor there had been. Peering past the pillars through the heavy rain that was now falling, I suddenly saw the Ghost Monastery.

It looked like a misshapen castle that had not been lived in for a very long time. The entire building seemed to be made of the same white marble as the pillars that I stood hidden behind, but some parts were so thickly covered with moss and vines that it was hard to tell which parts were a building and not a grassy hill. Two towers still stood intact, but even as I squinted at the castle, I swore I could see them crumbling. The double doors were made of wood, and a path lined with large, pointed rocks joined the marble pillars with the monastery.

"It doesn't much look like a monastery," I muttered, mostly to myself. Daya heard me, and replied, "The monastery was never actually a monastery—it used to belong to an ancient king, who ruled the mountains.

When he died, the monks came to collect spirits. Some say that they were men who had committed dreadful crimes, and in doing so had become nothing but evil spirits themselves."

"So the Force drove the monks out?"

"Oh no," Zharabi said grimly. "It imprisoned and tortured them. They are still in there, along with the many other souls that the Force has collected..."

There was a silence, during which I wondered if the Force had the spellbook.

"So if the Force does have the spellbook, how will we find it? Zharabi, do you think you could fly in to see if it's in there?"

The butterfly shook back and forth. "No. The Force is also a shapeshifter, so it will be able to detect my presence right away. If anyone was to go, it would have to be someone who was pure human—like you, Tien."

"Me?" I was horrified at the thought of going into the castle alone.

Daya snapped at Zharabi, "We all have to go! We can't let Tien go in alone..."

The butterfly bobbed up and down.

"Yes, we'll come with you."

I nodded, but the fear in my stomach only worsened as we slowly made our way toward the castle. At last, the doors loomed in front of us, larger than I could have possibly imagined. Engraved upon the chipped and splintered wood were lions and tigers fighting men. I looked at the battle more closely. The men were depicted to look vicious and bloodthirsty, but the animals looked angelic and almost godlike as they valiantly fought.

"He was a tiger," said Daya. I looked at her. "The king was a tiger?"

She nodded. I placed my trembling hand on one of the large black iron handles, and pushed. The door opened with a loud creak. I leapt back in fright, and landed on Daya's paw. She gently nudged me forward with her nose. I pushed the door open again, and it swung open fully, revealing a large entrance hall. Musty air blew into my face, and I inhaled it. Stifling a cough, I stepped inside the hall.

It was lit brightly by torches, whose flickering flames illuminated the various tattered tapestries adorning the walls. At the end of the entrance hallway, I spotted another set of double doors that were slightly open. Golden light spilled through them, and I was immediately drawn towards the doors.

"Daya, hurry!" Zharabi's whisper echoed through the hall. I turned, and saw Daya standing at the entrance, transfixed by the tapestries. She hurried down the hall as I pushed on the second set of doors. They fell open, and I found myself looking at a beautiful chamber.

The entire room had a mural running around it, similar to that of the tapestries. I could see that Daya was correct; the king had most certainly been a tiger, though I couldn't imagine how she had known this. The mural continued across the walls, floor, and even the ceiling. It was painted in a myriad of bright colors that reminded me of the rainbows I had searched for in the skies when I was a child.

In the center of the room was a large chair. It looked as though it was made of solid gold. I moved closer to it and marveled at the way the gold had been engraved with more images of the majestic tiger.

"Tien, look at this!" The butterfly was perched on a windowsill at the other end of the room. I walked across, looking up at the ceiling while I did so.

"The spellbook is in that tower." The butterfly used one of its delicate soot-colored wings to point out a tower some fifty feet away. Leading to the tower were crumbling stairs held above the sharp rocks far below by their frail connections to the castle and the tower itself. Inside the gray stone tower, I could see the spellbook. It was glowing with a faint gold light, and was suspended a few feet above a stone pedestal.

"It's beautiful, isn't it?"

I whipped around at the sound of a new voice. Leaning against the large door that I had pushed open only minutes ago stood a young man. He was about my age, but had fair skin, brown hair that stood stiffly upon his head, and dark eyes that were complemented by his all-black ensemble. I shivered when I looked at his eyes—silver threads appeared at the edges of his dark irises, creating an eerie glow.

Daya had moved next to me and bared her teeth as she studied the boy. Zharabi fluttered to my shoulder, and whispered, "Be careful. He is part of the Force."

The boy laughed. It was cold and chilling, like the rain that continued to fall outside the castle.

"Your protectors, I assume? A golden snow leopard, and a…" he paused here for effect. "…a moth?"

"Actually," I said quietly, "It's a butterfly."

"Quite right. A butterfly…but a black butterfly! How unusual that a creature is ever all black, don't you think? And yet look at me! I attempt to wear all black to blend with the night and the darkness."

The more the boy spoke, the less I liked him. His condescending tone reminded me of the children who used to tease me in the village. I crossed my arms and watched him, Rinzen and the sword still in my hand.

"Can your butterfly do tricks?"

The boy laughed mirthlessly when I did not reply.

"Perhaps I should have addressed that question to the butterfly itself! Can you do tricks, shapeshifter?" He spat the last word out bitterly. Zharabi left my shoulder, and transformed once more into the shape of a black panther.

"You guess well…Should I call you Lord of the Castle?" Zharabi's tone was polite, but it seemed to irritate the boy, who snapped, "It was no guess, you fool—it was magic! And I am Lord of the Castle, but I also have another name."

"I see." The panther smiled at the boy, but did not ask for his name. The boy watched us, and a long uncomfortable silence ensued. Finally, he spoke again, strolling around the room as he did so.

"You know, my father once said that there is no such

thing as coincidence—everything happens for a reason. He was right…My father was a great man. That is why he came here, to this country. After all what better achievement than conquering the unconquered, seeing the new world and taming it?"

He was walking along the mural that covered the far side of the wall as he spoke, not even looking at us. His slender hand ran along the paint on the wall as he walked, and I saw that silver electricity crackled from the tips of his fingers. A shock ran through my body that I recognized as fear. I chanced a quick glance out the window, but the ground looked painfully far away. That meant we had to make it to the door in order to find a way to the spellbook. But was there a way from the main hall?

My mind was working frantically, and a quick look at Zharabi and Daya told me that they were doing the same. The boy was now studying the mural, and had fallen silent for several moments.

"But I wanted more. For me, simply taming was not enough. No, I wanted power. I craved it from the very moment I set foot in this land. Power, freedom…together, those bring happiness…yes, that's right. How does one acquire power, and command it? And when I say power, I don't mean chief of the village power, like that fool Amir…no, I wanted to be magical."

He had strolled the full length of the room now, and now stood facing me, mere feet away.

"Magic is a strange thing. It's like a friend that eludes you and taunts you, but in the end if you can harness it,

the power it gives will reward you beyond your dreams."
He strode closer as he said it, and Daya, Zharabi, and I
backed up against the wall. The boy held out his hand and
said pompously, "I think I forgot to introduce myself. My
name is Austin Chancellor."

I did not take his hand. The boy's somewhat childish
smile vanished, to be replaced with a look of disgust.

"So you won't tell me your name? I already know
it—Tien Ming. I never managed to grasp how you
escaped my men not once but twice!" He held up two
fingers. I shrugged as casually as I could. This seemed to
irritate Austin.

"It isn't a matter you can shrug your shoulders at. Now
tell me: how did you do it? What magic did you use?"

I finally spoke. "I didn't use magic...I don't know any."

Austin stopped pacing long enough to shoot me a
nasty look. "Very funny, really. If you didn't know how to
use magic, how did you make it up the Steps of Death?"

"I walked."

Austin stopped pacing, and said angrily, "Fine. If this
is how you want it, I will indulge in your little mind
games...but first, let's see what we can do with your
friends, shall we?"

Raising his hands slowly, Austin shouted, "I call to
you, Master, to help me now!" To my horror, the silver
electricity that crackled at Austin's fingertips exploded
from his palm, and barreled towards Zharabi. The black
panther leapt out of the way, and attempted to transform,
but the electricity formed a silver cage which barred his

transformation.

"I think not," Austin said softly. "You thought you could fool me by becoming a butterfly? I miss not even the smallest traces of magic..." Without turning from Zharabi, who remained a panther, Austin opened his other hand, and imprisoned Daya in a similar silver cage. He laughed as Zharabi tried to shapeshift, failing every time. Tapping the side of the cage, Austin said happily, "Shapeshifter proof. I made it myself...brilliant, don't you think?" He stepped back as Zharabi shook the cage and growled at him.

"Temper, temper...I'll let you out eventually if you behave."

I snorted disbelievingly. Austin strolled away from Zharabi's cage, and towards me.

"You don't think I'm a man of my word?"

"No, I can't say that I do." I kept my voice even, and held my sword out. Austin put his hands up as if to show me his lack of weapons.

"You draw your sword, Tien! This is just a friendly conversation...isn't it?" Sitting down on the throne, he leaned back and surveyed the room at large, ignoring Daya's growls.

"Stop being so pompous," I snapped, irritated. Austin sneered at me.

"I suppose you think you could stop me. You think a lot of yourself, Tien, I can see it in your eyes...that feeling of self-righteousness that some get when they think they are helping others or the world at large." Leaning forward, Austin glared at me and then said in a low voice, "Learn this now, Tien. The spellbook is mine and mine alone. You will not take it from me. Go back to your village, and I will spare your life."

I grew angry when Austin spoke of my village.

"You killed Wise Woman. She was the only family I had! I have no home to return to, no family, and no life."

Austin sneered, "You never had any of those things to begin with! Family is an illusion I deprived you of. I took your father first. He was very easy to capture though he claimed to be a warrior—but he was a weak human, and easy to overpower."

Austin chuckled, as though he was remembering a particularly exciting gift he had gotten.

"Yes, I used a snowstorm for him. It was over quite quickly. Your mother was next. She put up a fight, and there was an infuriating owl that got in the way."

I glanced at Zharabi, now curled into a ball within the silver cage. Had he known my family? What was it that he had remembered back in Sangmu's hut when Rinzen had been formed? I felt frustrated as more unanswered questions continued to leap into my mind. Austin continued talking while playing with the silver electricity that ran through his very veins.

"But she was weak, your mother. Emotionally, of course, as well as physically. It was not difficult to overpower her, but she refused to give me the password to the spellbook. I was patient with her for months, but eventually I grew tired of her insistence on keeping the password hidden from me. She met the same fate as your father."

"And what fate was that?" I asked through gritted teeth, but Austin did not notice my tone. He replied carelessly, "I imprisoned her. Oh, no, they aren't dead. Merely imprisoned like your friends here." He gestured to Daya and Zharabi, who were both sitting docilely and watching Austin with the utmost loathing.

I nodded, thinking about where my parents were. Could they be kept in the room that Struptha had spoken about?

"But what good was the book without a password? I knew that your grandfather owned the spellbook and had created it, but it was not acquiring this book that concerned me. No, I was worried about how to get the password. For if the only people who held it could not be coerced and tortured into giving it up, what was I to do?" Austin stood up from the chair, and walked over to me, rubbing his hands together joyfully.

"So I captured your grandfather—surprisingly, he was the most difficult to ensnare with my magic. His guardian…" Austin spat this word out as though it was dirty, "protected him well. But in the end, not even a foolish black owl could overcome the power of the Force. I would have killed them both, but I…changed my mind."

"Why?" I asked loudly, but Austin ignored me. I was convinced now that Zharabi had been the owl. But why hadn't he mentioned it to me? Was there something else he was hiding?

"I brought the book here, but your grandfather refused to give up the password. Interestingly enough, I found that there was a family spat of some sort between your grandfather and mother." Austin smiled at me, his black eyes sparkling with joy. I looked at him, disgusted.

"Through this fight, I learned that there was one more member of the family whom I had been unaware of. You." Austin smiled at me and said cheerfully, "Well, of course, I was delighted. A mixed blood girl from a magical family...of course, this news was not good for the imbalance of power that I had worked so hard to achieve." Austin waited for my reaction, but I remained where I was, the expression on my face unchanging. Austin shrugged as though it did not matter to him whether I responded or not, and turned around so that his back was to me. He clasped his hands behind his back while he spoke, walking back towards his throne.

"And so, I waited. Patiently, I might add. I watched, as you grew up, slighted by the other children in your village. They did not see your power for what it was."

"Power? I don't understand...and you can't have captured my parents. You aren't any older than I am."

Shooting me a contemptuous look, Austin replied, "Of course I'm older than you. In two months, I will have lived two and a half decades. Ah yes, two months...The unity of the sun and moon will be around then, won't it?" Seeming to realize he had diverted from his original story, Austin continued to talk, enjoying the sound of his own voice.

"But Wise Woman was all too true to her name.

She told you the story of your family, over and over, and it drove me nearly insane! In addition to her teaching, you were unduly curious, and overheard the elders of the village speaking many times when you should not have. Naturally, it would have been my preference to see you when you were completely uneducated. Things took a good turn when Wise Woman passed away. I knew then that I must capture you, and take Wise Woman's soul so that she would not try to interfere. Unfortunately only one part of my plan worked." Austin shot me another nasty look, but I was only half listening to what he was saying.

I had to get out of the monastery as quickly as possible, but I was not willing to leave without Daya and Zharabi—and although I knew it was near impossible, I hoped to save my family. But where were they? If I made a break for the door, Austin would catch me and capture me. My only option was to keep him talking, something that was obviously not hard to do.

"So I retreated while you found the shapeshifter and leopard. I confronted you once more, but because of your friends, you escaped. When I learned you were going to find Rinzen, I was furious. I had imprisoned Sangmu, and you freed her. It seemed less and less likely that we could ever be partners."

"Partners? We were never going to be partners," I snapped, irritated by Austin's conceited attitude. He waved off my comment.

"A mere technicality. Coercion is sometimes the

beginning of a fruitful partnership." His eyes flicked to the cage where the black panther stood, alert and watchful, but returned to me so quickly that I thought I might have imagined it.

"I chased you that night, but once again, I was unsuccessful. And you escaped with Rinzen. So I returned here, to my hideaway, and waited for you to arrive." Austin gestured to the room from his throne.

"Are you coming to the point soon?" I attempted to sound as though Austin's speech were boring me. He smiled at me, and leaned forward in the throne.

"Work with me, and together we can use the spellbook to wipe out all the magical creatures that live in the mountains. Only one kind of magic will reign, and it will be a new magic, human magic.

"You were never accepted as a child, Tien. Don't you want to show the world what you can do? If we make the human race magical, there will be a new age in which we can be kings and queens!" The mocking tone had vanished from Austin's voice, and I realized, with a jolt in my stomach, that he was serious.

I listened to Austin's words, and looked at his childishly joyous face, but I knew as soon as he spoke that it would not work.

"But the magic wouldn't really be ours. It would be the Force's."

Austin shrugged and responded, "Power is power. We would be in command alongside the Force. Even now, the Force has given me amazing powers, and I can command and create as I would have never dreamed to have done before."

I shook my head. "I can't join you."

"Oh really? And why not?" Austin raised his eyebrows.

"You took away my chance to have a family, to have a proper life. When you were in the village where Sangmu lived, did you see those people? They were happy, truly happy, Austin—I could have had that life! But you stole it from me...I will never join you." My voice shook as I spoke, and Austin looked at me in disgust.

"You are weak to place value on family. A mistake that was once mine, but no more. I know the truth now—the only person you can rely on in your lifetime is yourself. But since you seem so reluctant to join me, I think I should teach you this lesson." Austin pushed back his sleeves, and I saw a gold watch in his hand. He glanced at it, and then smiled. "I have time, it seems, to show you your mistake, before I must go."

He held his right hand, palm up, in the air for a moment. Silver mist crept out of his palm, and swirled around until a shimmering silver blade had been made. It was a fairly large sword, with jewels set into the hilt. Austin gripped the sword in his right hand and said conversationally, "Shall we duel? I assume you would prefer without magic."

As he said this, he held out his left hand, and pushed it forwards. A band of silver light swept through the room like a wave, rattling the bars of the cages that Daya and Zharabi were trapped in. I was knocked off my feet, and Rinzen fell from my hand. Whispers of the shadows that had chased me after I had taken Rinzen filled the room, and I could see blackness creeping over the mural, covering the brave tiger's face until I could see it no longer. I held out my sword, watching the glowing silver blade as it danced across the room towards me. Austin's face was lit up by the glow from his blade. He cackled as he advanced slowly.

"Fear is a brilliant emotion. Don't you think so?"

"I can't say that I do." I spotted Rinzen on the ground, and picked it up. "Help me," I muttered.

"Talking to yourself already? Why, I..." Austin was cut off as violet flames erupted from Rinzen, lighting up the pitch-black room. I held the flower in the air, turning on the spot. Austin had been knocked backwards, and was slumped against the wall, the glow in his blade dulled slightly. His eyes opened, and I jumped back with fear—they had turned the same silver as his blade, making him look possessed. He stood up and brushed his clothes off mechanically, his luminous eyes never leaving me. I held Rinzen like a torch as Austin came towards me, swinging his blade wildly. I ducked the first swing, and sidestepped the second, but the third time he swung, I was forced to use my sword. Blocking his swing, I pushed him back, but Austin came forward again, relentless. Our swords hit once, twice, once, twice, in a rhythmic beat. I clenched Rinzen in my right hand, thoughts running through my mind more quickly than I could process them. I wanted more than anything to find the door, to escape the terrible shadows, but I had to distract Austin first. If I could make it into the main hall, there might be a staircase leading to the top of the tower, where we had seen the spellbook.

Austin's sword swung so fast that it soon became a blur in the air. His eyes remained silver as we fought, and he was no longer speaking, but I could feel the anger pouring from within him every time his blade connected with mine. Suddenly, he punched me, his fist colliding with my jaw. The movement was so unexpected that I had no time to defend myself. Stars danced in front of me, along with the blurry movement of the silver blade. I felt Rinzen fall from my hand, and was plunged into darkness once more.

I heard Austin kick Rinzen across the floor, somewhere in the distance behind me. I fell back onto the cold ground, trying to ignore the trickle of blood that had slowly made its way down the side of my mouth. My hands searched the floor frantically for the smooth stem of the flower, but all I could feel were the rough, cracked tiles of the ancient floor. Austin closed in on me, his face leering unpleasantly in the bright light from the silver blade.

"This is it, Tien," he panted. "This is the end. You should have joined me."

I continued to half slide, half crawl backwards across the floor, my hand still searching for Rinzen. I kicked out at Austin. He snarled angrily, and fell back. I scooted back, and suddenly felt the wall. My heart leapt and I scooted along the wall. *Please let the door come soon,* I thought.

Austin returned out of the darkness, and lunged at me. I yelled as he pressed his blade down onto my neck. My sword arm grew sore from the effort of keeping his blade away from me. Finally, I felt my fingertips close around the soft, velvety stem of a flower. I thrust Rinzen into Austin's face, and he roared as violet flames scorched his face. Scrambling up, I sprinted to the double doors, which were only a few feet away.

With Austin's cries still echoing in my ears, I ran back down the entrance hall. The torches had been extinguished, and my only source of light was Rinzen, its flames illuminating only a few feet in front of me.

"Come on! Show me the way to the spellbook!" I shouted at Rinzen. Austin's footsteps were echoing down the hallway. He was screaming at me.

"YOU WILL NOT ESCAPE ME! YOU WILL PAY!"

Violet flames showered a path to my left. I ran, and found a set of stone stairs, with more tapestries lining their walls. Running up the stairs as fast as I could, I heard Austin behind me, and could see his silver blade only a few stairs below me. Sprinting up the last few stairs, I found the doors at the top locked.

"No!" I gasped. Austin was drawing nearer. Bringing my sword down, I chopped at the rotting wooden doors. Kicking at the door, I made a hole large enough for me to climb through. Without looking back, I ran down yet another dark hallway. Opening the door at the end, I slipped through and quickly locked it behind me. I found myself at the foot of another set of curving stairs. I realized that I must be at the foot of the tower where the spellbook was kept. Still clutching Rinzen and my sword, I ran up the stairs, fearing that Austin would burst through the door at any moment.

At the top of the stairs was a large, round room. At one end was the window through which I had seen the spellbook, but it was not the spellbook that drew me into the room. Unlike the other rooms in the castle, this one was obviously well taken care of, and the rugs and tapestries were not ripped or moth-eaten. The spellbook stood in the center of the room, floating eerily a few feet above the pedestal. On the empty, dark wall behind the spellbook sprung images, so fast at first that I couldn't see what they were. Walking around the spellbook, I approached the images.

"I can't see them properly," I murmured, running my hand over the smooth wall. At once, Wise Woman's face appeared in it. She was a spirit, made of swirling white mist.

"Wise Woman!"

She smiled at me. "Hello, Tien."

"What are you doing...in the wall?" I touched the wall again, and her face became clearer.

"This is not actually a wall. It is an entrance to the Hidden Castle, the concealed part of this castle. It is here that the Force keeps the people and spirits it has captured. There is only one other entrance to this part of the building, in the depths of the Crystal River."

"What's the Crystal River?" I asked, but Wise Woman hushed me.

"Take the spellbook. You must take it, and return to the grove. You have done well, Tien, and I-I..." But something was going wrong. Wise Woman's face was fading from the wall, and she held out her hands to me, a panic stricken look upon her face.

"Wait! Come back!" I watched miserably as her face vanished. I stared glumly at the wall for a moment, and then suddenly felt immense pain as a blade pierced the side of my arm. I fell to my knees as the black boots of Austin Chancellor stepped into my line of vision. He bent down until he was at eye level with me, and whispered, "So sorry to interrupt the little family reunion. You barred the door quite well...it took me several minutes to get through it."

I yelled a mixture of inarticulate words, and swung my blade wildly. It scratched the side of Austin's face, and he wiped blood from his cheek, his eyes turning from black to silver as he did so. I pulled his blade out of my arm, and saw drops of bright red blood splatter onto the floor, staining the rug. Austin said to me quietly, "You'll pay for that." Standing up, he held out his palm, and drew it slowly upward. I felt my body being pulled upwards and I was thrown against the opposite wall. I saw Austin's shoes as he slowly made his way across the room, Rinzen glowing behind him. I propped myself up on one elbow, and rubbed my head. Austin raised his hands, and I could see the silver electricity crackling at his fingertips. As he brought his hands down, I knew I was defenseless, and closed my eyes in trepidation. As the white hot pain closed over me, I felt the world around me slowly go black.

Chapter Sixteen

The Crystal River

"Tien...Tien, wake up." Blurry images danced around my eyes. I shook my head, and squinted against the sudden bright light. Where was I?

"You're in the bamboo grove." It was Daya who spoke. She sat at the foot of the simple cot I lay on. Next to her sat a youth of my age whom I had never seen before. His eyes bore into my own, and I looked away quickly, disconcerted. The one-room house was simple. Bamboo reeds stretched to make the walls, roof, and door of the hut. In the far corner, under a window, was a simple and crudely whittled wooden table. Beyond the window I could see the comforting sway of the bamboo trees.

My gaze returned to the room. I looked at Daya. She smiled at me, her eyes glowing. I asked Daya, "How did you get out of there?"

She pointed to the boy. "He did it all. I can't claim any credit."

I nodded, and studied the boy. He was wearing simple cotton clothes, like the men in the village where we had met Sangmu. His clothes were cream and gold, and complemented his medium skin. He had dark hair that was unruly and stuck up in different directions. I thought him to be a stranger, but his dark eyes were familiar.

"Zharabi?"

He nodded, and enveloped me in a sudden hug. I could smell fresh grass and the sharp, tangy scent of bamboo. We broke away after a moment, and Zharabi said, "It's nice to be in human form for a change."

I wasn't listening, but trying to discern why I was blushing.

Zharabi sat down again, crossing his long legs. "It turns out transforming into a human broke my cage. I guess Austin wasn't expecting that. We got to the tower, and managed to stop him before he got you completely. You put up a good fight."

I nodded in acknowledgement. "Thanks. Did we get the spellbook?"

Zharabi shook his head. I leaned back against the headrest of the cot, feeling the rough bamboo absentmindedly.

"Don't look so dejected," Daya said kindly.

I ignored her, and asked, "What about Rinzen?"

Daya and Zharabi exchanged looks. I felt my heart sink as Zharabi said slowly, "You shouldn't blame yourself for losing Rinzen. It was inevitable; the flower would have been destroyed eventually."

"It's destroyed?" I cried out. Daya shot Zharabi a nasty look, and he held his hands up. Daya said quickly, "Rinzen would have been destroyed anyway, Tien. Now Sangmu has finally passed on forever."

"I guess so...but I wasn't able to find my family," I replied, the words stinging on my tongue as I spoke them. Disappointment washed over me, and a long silence transpired, during which no one spoke. Finally, Zharabi broke the silence.

"Now, about the spellbook," he began. "Austin will have moved it from the tower. Daya and I have talked about this, and we think he may have put it in the Crystal River."

"Wise Woman mentioned that to me," I said, and was suddenly reminded of the Hidden Castle. "I saw Wise Woman in that tower! She said that the wall is actually a portal to the Hidden Castle. That must be where the room is that Struptha told us about! She also told me that the only other entrance to the hidden castle is in the depths of the Crystal River."

"The Hidden Castle..." Daya paused, and Zharabi and I both looked at her. "My father showed it to me once. It was bewitched to never change. The castle itself is not very large, but I can imagine why Austin is holding his captives there."

"Why?" I was sitting straight up now, my feelings of lethargy gone.

"The Hidden Castle is heavily guarded by charms or enchantments. Its original purpose was to keep the monastery's inhabitants safe from invaders. Austin may not know about the entrance from the Crystal River, however."

"So if I enter the Crystal River, I can swim to the bottom and save my family!" I made to stand up, but Zharabi pushed me back down gently, laughing.

"It's not quite that easy." He glanced at Daya.

"It fills the whole room, and only the rocks that jut out of the river are sanctuaries of dry land. The Crystal River has existed for many years, in both legends and myths, but few have seen it," she said.

"For every person who enters the River, there is a crystal awaiting them. You will be drawn to the crystal, which contains the soul of a lost loved one. These crystals could be used to guard the spellbook, because if you touch one that is not yours, it will fatally wound you. Despite this, it might still be possible, but very difficult, for you to retrieve the spellbook if you were able to find your crystal...It would protect you from the others." Zharabi frowned as he spoke.

"Why would I struggle in finding my crystal?" Finding a crystal seemed like one of the easiest tasks I had been assigned throughout my strange journey.

"The river is twenty feet deep, and fierce currents can drown even the best swimmer. Forget that for now... I think Austin would have put the spellbook somewhere in the river, and will be waiting for Tien to come and get it," Daya spoke calmly.

"Why can't we go together?" I asked.

"The Crystal River is inaccessible to animals, or any magical being that is aware of its power. That is why its power is coveted by men. This means that the Force cannot reach the river, Tien, but you will still have Austin to contend with..." Zharabi's voice trailed off.

"We can only take you as far as the entrance to the Crystal River. There is a tunnel, and you must follow it. When you get to the river, do not get distracted by anything you might see. *Get the spellbook*." The urgency in Zharabi's voice worried me.

"What would distract me in the cave?"

"We don't know."

"Oh." I remained silent as we traversed the now familiar path toward the monastery. Instead of entering the monastery, however, we slipped into an almost invisible crevice, and I found myself looking down upon an amazing sight.

Torrents of golden water raged far beneath us in a large, dome-shaped tunnel. On the ceiling were paintings and engravings depicting the magnificent tiger that I had seen in the throne room. Small islands lay scattered throughout the water, their black surfaces wet from the constant splashing of water. On the other side of the large cave, I could see another small cliff, similar to the one we stood upon.

"This is it," said Daya over the noise of the rushing water. I stepped forward until my toes were over the edge of the cliff. Beneath me, the golden surface of the water seemed to become even fiercer, shining drops spraying the islands as the waves rose higher. Turning to look one last time at Zharabi and Daya, I jumped off the cliff.

My body fell quickly, and I shut my eyes tightly to avoid looking at the distance beneath me. After what seemed to be an eternity, I fell into the Crystal River, and sunk beneath the thrashing waves.

The water closed in around my head, and I kicked my legs frantically, and came up once more, gasping for air. The river continued on after the large island, but the tunnel curved, and I could not see where it led.

I allowed the current to pull me down the river until I reached the largest rock. I could see the spellbook suspended in midair in the center of the island, its binding glittering with a gold light. Gripping the slippery edge of the rock, I pulled myself onto the island, and stood up quickly, holding my sword ready. Slowly spinning around, I made sure the tunnel was empty before turning my attention to the center of the island. I approached the spellbook, and my hand was less than inch from it, when I sensed movement in the cave.

I already knew who it was, even before the voice sounded around the echoing chamber, and I was forced to turn around. Austin Chancellor stood behind me, clothes soaked, hair dripping. His sword was in one hand, just like mine. He was panting slightly, and I realized that he must have followed me into the cave.

"I see you found the spellbook. It took me some time to get here when I found out, but I came as fast as I could." Austin pushed me away from the center of the island. He dragged me to the edge, and forced me to look into the water around us.

"Do you see that water, Tien?" His voice was barely a hiss, but still sounded off the walls of the cave. I gritted my teeth, and pulled away from his grip. He kept talking.

"This water is not ordinary. It was cultivated by the monks, who used to practice the art of the dead in this monastery. At the bottom of the river are crystals like you have never seen before. They cover the riverbed so completely that if you were to walk on it, you would be pricked a thousand times over. The crystals are so powerful that they envelop any magical being. This has been perfect security for me, because normally no human dares to come onto the dark side of the mountain." Austin glared at me.

I blurted out, before I could stop myself, "So why don't they envelop you? Aren't you magical?" I wished I had not spoken when Austin looked at me, his eyes like cold ice.

"I am not a being of pure magic. I was once human... like you." His voice was full of contempt. I frowned.

"You don't have to be magical to stand out. You don't need the spellbook."

"Once I have the spellbook, I will have the secret to

immortality! No one, Tien, not even you, can stop me from achieving this goal." Austin's eyes flashed with a new insanity that I had not yet seen.

"Why do you want immortality so much, Austin? Wouldn't you rather live through only your given time on this earth, rather than living through every pain that the world goes through?"

"You don't understand, you foolish girl. If I am to live through all centuries on this earth, I will be able to have world domination and ultimate power! Isn't that what you would do?"

"No," I said quietly. "I would bring my family back to life. That's why I've wanted the spellbook from the beginning."

Austin seemed to contemplate what I had said for a moment. He looked mindlessly at the water, seeming to remember something from the past, something he didn't want to. His eyes flashed, and, for a moment, I thought I saw them turn blue. The next moment, they were black once more, and Austin was panting. I watched him closely. From the water running down his face, it was hard to tell, but were there tears mixed in? He shivered, and took a deep breath. Turning to me, he shook his head.

"You're a fool. Family is a waste of time! They give you no power!"

What happened next was so sudden that I was shocked by it. Austin crumpled, and fell to the ground, clutching at his hair, and kneeling on the ground, trembled. I did not need any magic to see that Austin was in terrible pain from something in his past. I wondered what had made Austin turn to magic as his refuge, to take away the pain.

He finally stopped trembling. For many moments, the only noises were the currents slapping the rocks. I began to walk toward the spellbook, hoping every moment that Austin would stay in his current state long enough to let me escape.

As I passed Austin, his hand shot out, grabbed my ankle, and pulled me to the ground. I landed with a bump on the smooth black rock. Grabbing my sword, I held it out. Austin sat up. All traces of humanity had vanished from his face, and his eyes had turned jet black once more. He grabbed the sword out of my hand. We wrestled it for a moment, but I let go as he bore his eyes into mine, causing me to be temporarily blinded. Standing up, Austin dragged me along the rock, by the wrist, to the edge of the island. Kneeling down, he pushed my head into the water.

I swallowed a mouthful of the water. To my surprise, it tasted like sweet honey, the one treat I had coveted in the village as a child.

I opened my mouth to drink more of the water in, but remembered the warning Daya and Zharabi had given me: do not be tempted. Was this temptation? I abruptly closed my mouth, trapping water within it.

As Austin pulled me out of the water, I spat my mouthful onto him. Leaping up, I ran towards the spellbook, seeing nothing else. He was close on my heels, but I reached the spellbook moments before he reached me.

My hands closed around the worn leather binding, and I wrenched the book off the pedestal.

Not turning to look at Austin, I ducked two of his sword blows. At the edge of the island, I was about to leap, when I saw my sword fly over my head and land in the water. To my horror, it sank beneath the surface. Turning around, I saw Austin coming towards me, sword in one hand, ready to kill me. I knew I had only one choice. Taking a deep breath, I dove into the water after my sword.

As the water closed in around the top of my head, I searched the water frantically until I spotted it, sinking to the bottom of the river. I began to swim down to the bottom, the growing pressure making my ears feel as though they would burst any moment. Finally, I grasped my sword gratefully, and watched the crystals glimmer closer than ever. I picked up a particularly shiny one.

It was the length of my palm, and shone as I turned it in my hand. Grabbing the sword, I put the tip of the crystal into my mouth on instinct and bit down upon the smooth surface to keep it in place. I found myself able to breathe, and looked up at the top of the water. I began the slow swim up to the top, no longer worried about the distance.

As soon as my head broke onto the surface, I spat the crystal out, and pulled myself up onto one of the smaller rocks that led to the island where the spellbook was held. As I jumped from one rock to the next, sword still in hand, I saw Austin scramble up onto the largest island. He snatched the spellbook, and whooped gleefully.

"Give me the spellbook, Austin!" I shouted. He nearly jumped with shock and fright when he saw me.

"Come and get it, then!" He jumped off the island, and was carried downstream. I watched as he turned a corner and vanished from sight. I threw myself into the warm water and followed him. The powerful current pulled me along like a pair of immensely strong hands. I could see Austin's head bobbing in the distance. He turned to me and shouted, "You will never escape the river!" With those final words, he sank under the water. I ducked my head, and saw his body sucked underneath the crystals. I swam down to follow him, but was thrown back by the crystals. Returning to the surface, I allowed the currents to carry me along the river until I could see the end.

A wooden door stood at the end of the Crystal River. The water sloshed against it, wetting the already soaked wood even further. I spotted an iron ring that I assumed was a door handle. As the current propelled me into the door, I lunged at the iron ring, and gripped it securely with my fingers. Bracing my feet against the wall under-water, I pulled on the iron ring, and the door fell open. I swung myself onto cold stone stairs, and crawled up them. The door swung shut automatically behind me, leaving me in a dark stone tunnel, lit up by black torches.

I walked along the tunnel until I found myself at a fork. Two sets of stairs led in different directions, one to the right and in the direction of the monastery, and one directly ahead to the back of the monastery. Resisting the urge to explore the path that led straight, I took the path leading right, and jogged up the stairs.

Austin was at the end of the entrance hall, but he did not see me. I shrank back slightly and watched as he entered the throne room. He spoke to someone, imperiously. I tiptoed along the hallway, and pressed my ear to the door to listen.

Chapter Seventeen

The Shapeshifter's Betrayal

Austin found himself sucked through the crystals, as he had hoped. The next moment, he was being propelled underground, the water rushing all around him. Finally, he landed outside the monastery, covered in dirt and soaked from head to toe. Spitting out water, Austin brushed himself off, and strolled quickly and quietly along the path that led around the Ghost Monastery, the spellbook in his right hand. He hummed to himself, occasionally checking his strange gold watch. Pushing open the large double doors, Austin strode down the entrance hall and into the throne room once more. His brow furrowed when he saw a hunched figure sitting upon the golden throne in a brooding manner.

"You're late." Zharabi looked up.

"Oh, shut up," snapped Austin. "Don't act so high and mighty with me, you stupid shapeshifter. You know I have the upper hand. Now what have you got to tell me?"

Zharabi considered this question for several moments while Austin tapped his foot loudly on the floor.

"I'm not sure what you want me to say, Austin."

"Oh, come on!" Austin threw up his hands exasperatedly. "You mean to tell me that you didn't find out the password, after all this time? It was your job, as we discussed. Don't you remember the consequences?"

"Of course I remember the consequences!" Now it was Zharabi who stood up agitated. "And you won't lay a hand on anyone in Tien's family until my time is up." Austin rolled back his sleeve to reveal the gold watch. It had a sun and a moon engraved upon it, and with every second that ticked by, they drew closer. Austin pushed the watch close to Zharabi's face and hissed, "Well, take a good look, shapeshifter, because your time is almost up." Coming closer to Zharabi, Austin gripped him by the collar, and said menacingly, "That was a clever trick you pulled, transforming into a human. You knew you couldn't continue to shapeshift if you did so, but you were willing to risk it to save Tien. You fool." Turning away, Austin laughed.

"I ran from Tien you know, and I left her in the Crystal River, trapped. I feel like a fool, running from a little girl."

"Tien isn't a little girl. She's powerful, more so than you and I."

"That's a lie!" Austin shouted these last words. Zharabi simply replied, "Sangmu named her as the next Sorceress to rule the dawn of a new age."

"What? What did you say?" Austin's eyes were wild and full of silver streaks that crept across his pupils and irises slowly as he spoke.

"Don't pretend like you didn't know, Austin. Of course you knew, we all knew! She was destined to be the next great Sorceress from birth. And you contributed to it." Austin's face registered nothing but shock. He said angrily "And just how did I contribute to this?"

"You took Tien's family from her. Sangmu had her pick of mixed-blood children who came from magical families. There were many others, after all, although they may not have known it. But Sangmu chose Tien to be the next Sorceress because of her childhood. Tien was tormented by other children as Sangmu had been. You created that childhood by taking her family."

Austin's eyes narrowed. "You seem to have a very good memory, Zharabi, considering it was wiped clean the night you swore to help me get the book's password to save your master's life."

Zharabi shrugged. "I suppose Rinzen had a part to play in that."

There was a sharp intake of breath. Austin stamped his foot in frustration. "I knew it! Sangmu used her final powers to help you. How much do you remember?"

Zharabi met Austin's silver eyes unflinchingly. "Everything," he said quietly.

"I see. Well then, you won't mind if I wipe your memory clean once more...." Austin raised his hands, but Zharabi shook his head, and raised one hand. Austin was thrown back several feet.

"Fine," he snarled at Zharabi. "You can keep your memory, but I want the password from the girl! Now, is there anything else you would like to tell me...something about the strange shell she has hung around her neck?"

Zharabi nodded slowly. "Struptha gave it to her."

"The dragon?" Austin's eyebrows raised in disbelief. "All the dragons are dead. I checked the pass myself."

"He hid from you," said Zharabi hollowly. Austin growled with fury.

"So there must be other animals hiding in the mountains then...I wonder how many more have survived?" Sitting down in the throne, Austin dismissed Zharabi with a wave of his hand.

"You can go now Zharabi. We will meet again soon, I imagine."

Zharabi turned from the throne, and saw Tien leaning against the double doors, her sword in her hand.

"So...anything either of you would like to tell me?"

Chapter Eighteen

A Duel in the Monastery

Austin recovered first. He laughed and said, "Please, Tien, come in. We were just having a chat."

"Yes, I noticed." I walked into the room and faced Austin in his throne. He said to me, "It's rather a pity you didn't accept my earlier offer of partnership."

"What did you need me for when you had him?" I pointed to Zharabi without looking at him. He opened his mouth to speak, but Austin smiled at me.

"He is nothing but a shapeshifter. I admit, yes, that is a good talent to have and Zharabi does have some powers…but you are the next Sorceress."

"So I heard, but I don't think that's true…I am not

magical the way Sangmu was. In fact, I don't even want that position. You can have it, Austin."

He snorted. "It's not that simple. I can't take it from you now that you've been named by Sangmu. Fortunately, there is another option."

"I don't want to hear about your options," I snapped, but Austin continued anyway, speaking over me.

"If I could appease you now, and give you time to settle your affairs and business with this world, we could arrange it so that you joined Wise Woman...peacefully."

"You're telling me killing me is another option?" I had to laugh. Austin shrugged and stood up, the familiar glowing silver blade forming in his hand.

Zharabi tried to speak.

"Tien, you have to understand, this isn't what it looks like..."

"I don't need to hear your excuses right now," I said flatly, my eyes still focused on Austin, as I attempted to push away the churning of anger, sadness, and guilt that had suddenly risen in my stomach. Then suddenly, I dropped my hands and said, "You know, you're right, Austin. How does this option work?"

Austin laughed gleefully. "I knew you would see the light eventually!" I glanced at Zharabi and saw that he looked horrified.

"Tien, what are you doing?"

"Shut up," I muttered angrily.

As Austin turned away from me to return to the throne, I drew my sword, and kicked him in the back. He whirled around as he fell down, and drew his own sword once more out of thin air. Austin stood up, and swung his sword around at me. I leapt out of the way quickly, and his blade passed through the air uselessly. We circled slowly for a moment. I moved cautiously, my eyes never leaving Austin's sword.

He quickly dodged forward, but I was ready for him. I grabbed his wrist and twisted it. Austin cried out and dropped his sword, while I kicked him away. I grabbed his sword, and held the two swords out. Crossing the blades, I pulled them apart, and backed Austin into the wall. I held the swords to his throat, and pressed the blunt end of the blade into his neck as a warning. Austin's eyes were frightened, and, for a moment, I almost dropped the swords. However, as he began to struggle, I pressed them harder against his throat.

"Don't move," I snarled angrily.

"Or what?" Austin's voice was raspy.

"I'll slit your throat. I won't ever let you have the spellbook. In fact, I could just kill you now and take it from you...then nothing would matter anymore, would it?" I was breathing heavily, and a strange sense of happiness ran through my body, making me tremble violently.

I pulled my sword closer against Austin's neck. His eyelids fluttered in fear...and then out of nowhere, Zharabi's strong brown arms were around me, pulling me away from Austin.

"ZHARABI, LET GO!" I shouted angrily and tried to pull away, but Zharabi held tightly to my waist. I dropped the swords in my effort to pull free.

"LET GO OF ME!" I squirmed out of Zharabi's grip and grabbed the swords. Austin continued to sit on the stones, in a trance, his mouth agape at my newfound anger. Zharabi sprinted after me, and tackled me to the ground. He pulled me up, and we continued to fight.

"Tien, stop! Don't hurt Austin!" Zharabi tried to implore me as I fought him like a madwoman, only intent on one thing: killing Austin. I leapt out of his grip, and ran to Austin, but Zharabi hauled me back, and grabbed my wrist. We fought over the sword for a moment, but he finally ripped it out of my hand, and threw it across the floor. I fell back onto the floor as Zharabi stood panting, holding one of the swords. I scrambled up, and made my way towards Austin one last time. Zharabi grabbed me, and pulled me back with amazing strength.

Before I could scream or fight, Zharabi clapped a hand over my mouth, and spoke to me in a low urgent voice.

"You will not win this battle! Do not provoke him, it..."

I pushed Zharabi away and snapped, "Don't talk to me about battles! You've been fighting for the other side all along. And everything you said to Daya about being trust-worthy, when all along YOU were the one we shouldn't have trusted. Maybe Daya was right...never trust a shapeshifter..."

"Give me a chance to explain first!" Zharabi exclaimed.

"Explain what? Your battle tactics you planned out

with him?" I pointed a finger accusingly at Austin, who was still slouched against the wall. His eyes were beginning to glow silver again, and he raised his hand, and shouted, "Master, come now! Help me!"

A bitterly cold wind began to blow. I snatched my sword from Zharabi and sprinted across the room to Austin, reaching out my hand to snatch the spellbook from him, but a strong force threw me back. I landed on the ground, the blade clanking against the hard stone, and watched in horror as the wind picked up and began to form the shape of a woman in a silver cloak. I scrambled up, and ran out of the throne room. Zharabi followed me, his footfalls echoing in my head.

Another vibration ran through the ground, nearly cracking the floor. I ran out of the monastery and past Daya, who was standing by the white pillars. As we sprinted down the Steps of Death, I was finally able to see why no human had ever dared to cross them.

The bones that had littered the steps on our way up were now forming skeletons of all kinds, which leered at us unpleasantly. They came forward, and I dodged one's arm. Whacking it on the head with my sword, I watched as it spun around, dazed. Then, nearly tripping over my feet in my hurry to make it down the steps, I jumped over the other vibrating bones, dodged the forming skeletons, and finally jumped off the last few stairs. Daya, and then Zharabi landed next to me. We turned to watch as the skeletons tottered towards us, but were forced to stop at the bottom of the steps, where the realm of the Ghost

Monastery ended. Eventually, the vibrations stopped, and the bones crumpled up into piles once more.

"Did you get the spellbook?" Daya's voice was anxious. I shook my head, and said, "I would have taken it from Austin, but the Force arrived, and we had to run."

Zharabi spoke for the first time since we had left the monastery. "We have to go. Austin and his men could be anywhere."

He stood up to leave, but I blocked his way.

"You are not coming with us."

Daya looked confused. "Why not?"

"Why don't you tell her," I said to him. Zharabi opened his mouth, but seemed unable to speak. I waited then said to Daya in a shaking voice, "He made a deal with Austin Chancellor. He's been working to get the password from me this whole time."

Daya shook her head in disbelief. "Is this true?" she asked him. Zharabi sat down on the Steps of Death, and put his head in his hand. Daya looked at him, disgusted.

"Never trust a shapeshifter," she said quietly. "Come, Tien." She loped away down the path. I followed her, stopping only once to look at Zharabi, who sat at the foot of the Steps of Death, his head still in his hands.

Chapter Nineteen

The Sacred Forest

Our journey away from the monastery took us high into the mountains once more. The snow here was pure white, but had begun to melt slowly, running in tiny streams down the sides of the rocks that shaped the mountains. All around us, birds flew excitedly, chirping in delight at the bright sun and newly blossomed bushes. We traveled until nearly a month before the sun and moon would unite.

During this time, Daya and I grew closer, and I learned more about her life.

"My father was a tiger, and my mother was a leopard. They ruled over these mountains at one time…that was before the Force."

"I'm sorry they aren't here anymore."

Daya smiled at me. "My mother passed away naturally, but my father was killed..." She trailed off, and I did not press the point. As we continued to walk, she suddenly said to me, "Do not blame Zharabi for what he did."

"Why not? He deserves to be blamed for how he betrayed us," I said bitterly. Although it had been a long time since I had last seen Zharabi sitting against the Steps of Death, his head in his hands, I still felt a mix of emotions whenever we spoke about him.

"Where are we going?" I asked, desperate to change the subject.

"The Sacred Forest."

"Where Sangmu lived?" I felt excitement rush through me.

"I used to live there too," replied Daya. "After my family was gone, Sangmu took me in and cared for me. She did it for all animals that had no family."

Our final destination was something more beautiful than I could have ever imagined. Unlike my surroundings, which were white with patches of green, the valley we were to stay in was completely green. The dying sun shone on the treetops of the forest. I could see a waterfall in the distance, rushing down into a large pond. The grass was a dark, luscious green, and felt soft to touch.

We set up camp in a cave at the heart of the valley. That night, Daya spoke to me about the spellbook.

"There is something that perhaps I should have told you when I first met you..."

"What is it?" I prompted her. She hesitated then spoke again.

"After I attacked your mother but was driven away by Li Shen, I followed them to the grove, where I waited for my chance to attack. I saw your grandfather force your father to take you and leave…and then he told your mother the key to the spellbook."

"What was it? What was the key?" I asked eagerly.

"It…" Daya was no longer at ease, however. She stood and peered out into the night from the mouth of the cave.

"Someone is out there." Her eyes narrowed, as she tried to discern shapes through the faint light of the stars that spattered the sky. I picked up my sword, and joined her at the mouth of the cave.

"Should we go out and see who it is?"

Daya shook her head. "They're coming in this direction." Sure enough, I could hear the noise of feet against grass. I recognized the figure's gait even in the distance.

"It's Zharabi, isn't it?"

Daya nodded, and spoke to the figure in the distance. "We've already recognized you, so there's no point in trying to hide."

"I wasn't trying to," replied Zharabi. He moved into the ring of light given off by the fire in the cave. The shadows on his face made him appear sinister. I crossed my arms.

"What do you want?" Daya was sitting and surveying Zharabi curiously.

"I just wanted to explain. I'm not working for Austin.

The deal I made with him was a long time ago...Daya, please understand!"

Daya hesitated. "Sangmu told me your story, so I suppose I believe you. I don't understand why you did it, however...but I never had a master, or one to be devoted to for that matter."

Zharabi looked relieved and smiled gratefully at Daya. As he bent down to hug her, I slipped out of the cave.

The valley was even more beautiful in the night. The moonlight bathed every blade of grass, every tree trunk, and every leaf in a silvery sheen. I walked away from the cave, taking in the forest on my left, and the large rock wall on my right. Up ahead I spotted a large circle of trees, within which I could hear the rushing of water.

Suddenly, a slight noise behind me made me start. Turning around, I scanned the path behind me, but nothing was there. The grass swayed peacefully as a light breeze blew. Leaves blew down from the tops of the large trees. Flowers danced with the wind. I was unable to make out any noise or sound. My heart still thudding from the shock, I entered the clearing.

The waterfall rushed down the large rock wall into a pool, making the water frothy. Smooth gray boulders bordered the pool, some large enough for me to sit on comfortably. I heard another rustle behind me, and turned around, my sword pointing at Zharabi's heart.

"Put your sword down, Tien." He waited, but I did not lower my blade.

"Why don't you pull out your own sword? Then we can fight."

I swung my blade at Zharabi and he jumped backwards, out of the way.

"Tien, come on! Put the sword down."

I shook my head, and said, "Why don't you tell me how this deal came about, and then I'll put the sword down."

Zharabi nodded. "All right...but I think I should start at the beginning, when I was a boy." He raised his arms, and images appeared on the waterfall in front of us. I turned to watch, but did not lower my sword.

An image of my old village sprang up. I felt tears come to my eyes as I saw the children playing, and Wise Woman's hut. I continued to watch as Wise Woman herself came out of her, holding a little boy by the hand. I was confused for a moment, but when I saw Zharabi's face, I understood. A lone tear ran down his face as he watched Wise Woman take care of the boy, and nurture him.

The original images faded, and were replaced by one of the boy at an older age, perhaps five or six. He was climbing through the mountains, and came across a beautiful garden. He ran excitedly back to Wise Woman, and pulled at her, but she seemed reluctant to enter the garden. He could not persuade her to enter the garden, and she could not persuade him to leave it.

As the boy entered the garden, the sunny day turned dark, and a howling wind blew his hair around his face. Wise Woman ran after him, but found that she was nearly too late. The boy lay almost lifeless on the ground, deep cuts all over his body. As the boy remained still in the growing pool of blood, Wise Woman picked him up, and carried him out of garden.

The next image was in the grove. I saw Wise Woman chanting, and I suddenly knew where Zharabi had learned the strange song he had sung to me. Wise Woman chanted for a long time. Then, with a dramatic sweep of her hands, she mouthed, *"May you become more magical and powerful than those who have hurt you. Fly with the wind."* A mist covered the boy's face, and he vanished. There was a sudden burst of light, and Wise Woman was standing alone on the rock in the grove, watching a large black owl fly away. Tears fell down her face, as she put her hands together and prayed for the boy she had healed and changed to help him survive.

Zharabi turned to me. I shrugged. "What's the significance of any of that? You were made into a shapeshifter by Wise Woman."

"Yes...but she could not grant me the same luxuries as the others of my kind. Because I had been wounded as a human before I was made into a shapeshifter, I could not turn into a human for I would lose my powers if I did so. A human form was my weakest state, and would therefore turn me to a mortal if I took on such an appearance."

"Then why did you change to your human form?" I asked Zharabi. "Don't you miss the freedom of shape-shifting?"

To my surprise, he shook his head. "It is a relief to be returned to the body I once had, but without the scars I received that day in the enchanted garden of the Force."

I nodded, and then asked, "What happened after Wise Woman granted you the powers of a shapeshifter?"

Zharabi replied, "When I flew away, I went to your grandfather's village, and he became my master. I protected him when Austin came for the spellbook..." Zharabi raised his hands once more, and another scene played across the waterfall, the images crisp and clear.

An old man sat peacefully, working at his desk. I would not have recognized him if Zharabi had not cried out. I gasped as I saw a familiar black owl perched on the man's chair—the man must have been my grandfather.

The door of the hut burst open, and the men clad in black that had come for Wise Woman came for my grandfather. He stood, and bowed respectfully to the men. Austin stepped forward. He spoke to my grandfather, and although I could not hear what he was saying, I understood.

"He wants the spellbook," I murmured to myself.

My grandfather shook his head, and sat back down. Austin angrily pushed my grandfather off the chair, and drew his sword. Holding it to my grandfather's throat, he spoke again. My grandfather only shook his head, his dark eyes blazing with determination. Austin raised his sword in anger.

"No!" I cried out, forgetting that I was only watching the scene. Zharabi caught my arm to stop me from touching the waterfall. I looked at his face; he was pale. I realized that this must have been what Zharabi could not remember.

As Austin raised his sword to kill my grandfather, Zharabi, in the form of an owl, rushed forward, his wings beating. Scratching Austin across the face with his sharp talons, I saw Zharabi's beak open in a shrill cry. Looking murderous, Austin withdrew a sharp black stone from his cape, and hurled it at Zharabi. It hit him in the wing, and he twirled in midair, struggling to move. As he fell to the ground, Austin made to hurl another stone at him, but my grandfather caught Austin's arm. From behind the desk, my grandfather removed the spellbook. With shaking hands, he handed it to Austin, who snatched it greedily, his silver eyes shining with an intensity that frightened me. Grabbing my grandfather, he dragged him out of the hut, leaving Zharabi alone on the floor of the hut.

I still had not lowered my sword. Zharabi turned to me, and asked, "Do you understand?"

"But you weren't taken by Austin...Why did you make the deal?"

Zharabi said quietly, "I knew that Austin would kill my master and his family. I had heard your grandfather speak of how much he missed his daughter, and I wanted to save them all. So I traveled to the Ghost Monastery, and spoke with Austin..." Zharabi gestured to the waterfall, and I saw another series of images. Zharabi and Austin stood in the throne room, Zharabi as a black panther imprisoned in a metal cage. Austin was laughing and talking to the panther, whose dark eyes were blank.

"Austin took my memory from me," said Zharabi. "He then proceeded to tell me about you, and how you were living with Wise Woman. Because he had stolen parts of my early memories, I did not know that Wise Woman had saved me as a child, and given me the powers of a shape-shifter. If I had known, I would have told her immediately. Austin kept me inside a metal cage until I finally managed to persuade him to let me out. I said if I could find the next sorceress and acquire the password, he would set my master and his family free. Austin agreed, and set me free to come and find you."

"So that means you've known this from the beginning!" I swung my blade, but Zharabi grabbed my wrists, and we struggled for several moments before he grabbed my blade and flung it aside. I balled my hands into fists, and shouted, "Let go!"

"Not until you stop trying to hurt me!"

I glared at Zharabi and backpedaled furiously, trying to free my arms from his grip. We toppled into the pond at the foot of the waterfall. I spluttered, and pushed my hair out of my eyes. Zharabi spat out water, and said, "Well, at least you stopped trying to hit me."

I looked at him distrustfully. Zharabi said, "I'm telling the truth. I was trying to buy myself more time...Austin was getting impatient. I would have never given him the password...I couldn't have."

Zharabi took my hand as he spoke. I looked into his eyes suspiciously, but saw no sign that Zharabi was lying.

"I'm sorry I tried to fight you," I finally said. He shrugged, and replied, "I've had worse happen to me."

I grinned at him, and was about to ask what could

have been worse, when a golden glimmer in the pond caught my eye. I reached my hand into the cold water, and picked up a heavy gold pocket watch.

"I wonder whose it is," I said quietly, examining the watch.

Zharabi stood up, and said, "We should show Daya."

I nodded, and we exited the clearing together, leaving only the moonlight behind.

Chapter Twenty

Revelations

I showed Daya the watch I had found in the waterfall the next morning. She gasped.

"Where did you get that?" Her voice was hushed and fearful.

"It was at the bottom of the waterfall. I've seen this watch before," I said. I knew the time had come to tell Daya and Zharabi the vision I had seen with the vicious tiger and the death of the little boy's father. There was a silence after I finished my tale. Then Daya spoke, her voice heavy with emotion.

"The tiger was my father, who once reigned over this forest, but not anymore. He would not have killed the man if there had been no reason. That watch was in his mouth when we found him... that man must have been evil. You merely viewed the incident from the wrong point of view." Daya shivered, remembering memories from her past.

"I'm sorry about your father," I said quietly. Daya smiled sadly at me.

"Everything happens for a reason, Tien...his destiny was to die at the hands of that man."

I paused, thinking. If the man that I had seen was Austin's father, and the tiger was Daya's father...that must have meant that Austin was the boy who had been taken over by the Force without any warning. Was Austin really evil? Images ran through my mind of Austin's eyes flashing when I spoke of family. I remembered Wise Woman's words, and wondered if Austin was really the evil I should have been fighting for the return of the spellbook so I could bring my family back to life. Shouldn't we have fought the actual Force? The doubt of which evil I was fighting worried me. I gasped when I thought of what would happen if Austin refused to allow the Force to bend his mind any longer. I remembered how his eyes had flickered when I had spoken of family, how he had almost resisted the Force's magic. I stood up. Zharabi and Daya exchanged quizzical looks.

"Tien, where are you going?" Zharabi waited for my response.

"I'm going back to the monastery. I need to help Austin."

"Are you mad? Why would you want to help Austin?" Daya sounded incredulous. I paced up and down the cave while I spoke.

"When I was in the Crystal River with him, I talked to him about family and the importance of it. His eyes flickered, and he almost resisted the Force's power! He almost escaped, and if he thought any more about what I said I'm sure he will fight the Force. We have to help him!"

"But how do you know he isn't evil?" Daya protested. I stopped, and thought about it.

"I don't exactly know how…but he has traces of humanity. Austin isn't the Force—he's being controlled by it. If we free him, then we can fight the actual Force and destroy it!" I ran to the edge of the cave, but Daya and Zharabi stood hesitantly. I looked and them and said stubbornly, "I'm going no matter what. Now are you coming or not?"

They both nodded.

"We will come with you…but we need a plan first." Daya faltered when she saw my face.

"There isn't time for a plan!" I grabbed my bag, and ran up the side of the valley. Daya and Zharabi ran after me, crying out.

"Tien, wait! We have to plan how to help Austin!"

I stopped at the top of the valley.

"We might not get there in time, and timing is very important…I've just understood. All along, we have been battling the wrong evil. Everything is connected, all of us, this whole story. You, Zharabi, worked for my grandfather, who was hurt by Austin, whose father killed Daya's father. As a result of this, Daya attempted to kill my mother, which led to my mother meeting my father, Li Shen." I scrambled over rocks and continued to run down the slippery, slushy paths, with Daya and Zharabi tailing me.

"Why does the timing of our freeing Austin matter?"

"If we don't get the spellbook and free him before the sun and moon unite, either he will be captive for the rest of his life, or we will be destroyed! Austin has a father, he has a family—we just have to remind him of it. I think the watch we found should do it."

"I think I understand!" Daya was jubilant. Zharabi nodded and said in a grim tone, "We will have to see who survives and who does not. I think…"

What Zharabi thought, exactly, I never found out, because there was a tremor that shook the earth with such force that I fell to the ground. Picking myself up hurriedly, I felt another boom come from the direction of the dark side of the mountain. On my right and left, stood Daya and Zharabi, their faces taut with fear as we watched the dark clouds gather.

"We have to hurry," said Daya. And with that, we began to run across the rocky terrain towards the monastery, each of us not sure what to expect next.

Chapter Twenty-One

A Fight for Power

Austin pushed open the slightly rotted door to the hidden castle, leaving it ajar behind him.

"Where are you?" He addressed his words to the hall in general.

"Enter."

The voice came from the door at the end of the hall. It was by the sloping staircase. Austin slowly proceeded towards the door, feeling his feet beg to return to the monastery, where he could hide from the terrible Force. He was no longer sure of what he wanted; the power that he was being given suddenly no longer seemed to be making him stronger; in fact, it now felt like shackles against his body, weighing him down. Austin felt fear as he had never felt before rush through his body, making him feel sluggish and slow.

Pulling at the small blue door, Austin entered a domed room. Sharp silver crystals protruded from the walls and floor of the room, forcing Austin to stop at the entrance.

"Hello?" He spoke hesitantly now.

"You sound fearful." The Force materialized in the center of the crystals as a young woman, wearing a black robe identical to Austin's.

"No...I feel tired. Heavy. There's too much power." Austin slouched as he spoke. He muttered, "Maybe if you could take some away...it's so heavy."

"Why is it heavy? You have never complained of this before." The woman eyed Austin carefully.

"I don't know why," mumbled Austin, feeling weaker than ever. The woman's eyes narrowed, and she snarled, "He has returned."

"What are you talking about?" Austin's eyes were half closed. The woman screeched, "Your father is gone! You discarded him, cut him out of your heart...but he has returned. I can feel it." She quickly stole a glance around the room, as though half expecting Austin's father to appear out of nowhere.

Forcing his eyes to open, Austin said, "Please, take some of the power! I'm weak..." He fell to his knees. The woman snapped, "Get up, you fool. Rid yourself of the love! It is tampering with the power..." Raising her hands, she drew them back, and silver threads came out of Austin's heart, towards the woman. She caught them in her hand, and watched as Austin looked up, alert once more. His eyes were still black, but flickered to blue.

"You are ruining the magic! Control yourself, rid yourself of the love!" The woman's voice echoed around the crystal-filled room. Austin slowly raised his eyes to meet the Force, but he did not see the woman as a mentor any longer. The only images that filled his mind were ones of his father spending time with him, helping him to write, read, playing with him as a young boy.

"Father, where are we going?" The boy looked at his father adoringly as they walked across a cornfield.

"Do you remember the story I told you?" The man looked down at his son.

"The one about the tiger?" The boy clapped his hands together eagerly. "Father, are we going to see a tiger?"

The man laughed, and scooped up the little boy. Lifting him high into the air, the man said, "If we are lucky, we might see one. But remember, you must be quiet, otherwise we won't."

The little boy nodded, wide-eyed. "I'll be so quiet, even you won't be able to find me!"

The man smiled and said, "Not that quiet! I wouldn't be happy it if I couldn't find you."

"I would be sad too," the boy said with an admiring smile. The man put him down on the ground, and the two walked on through the cornfield, the boy gripping his father's hand tightly so as not to lose him.

"STOP!" The Force bellowed angrily. But Austin found that he could not stop. His childhood returned to him, and he breathed deeply, and closed his eyes. He smiled, and then laughed...and, finally, Austin realized that he no longer wanted to possess power. He opened his eyes, which were slowly, very slowly, changing back to blue.

Glancing down, he saw that the silver threads which had previously been entering his very heart were now shooting out across the room, and unraveling as though they were mere pieces of string. Even as Austin watched them, the silver threads dissolved into thin air, leaving no trace of their existence behind. Austin's eyes widened with fear as he saw the Force raise her hands, and move them backwards, the silver electricity crackling at the long, thin fingertips.

As more silver streams of light shot towards him, Austin closed his eyes, and prayed that he would not be consumed by the magic that had controlled him for so long. In his mind's eye, Austin could see his father again, always patient and caring for his only son. Austin felt warmth creep around his heart, thawing the icy block that the Force's magic had made it for so long. Opening his eyes, Austin raised his arms to the ceiling of the crystals, and cried out with happiness.

Looking around, he saw the silver beams writhing as though they were long serpents, thrashing in great pain. As Austin took a deep breath, the serpents vanished. From within his body, Austin saw silver serpents pouring; they flew out of his ribs, cheeks, and even legs as he laughed with joy to be returned to his true self.

The woman's eyes were wide with fury as she watched,

powerless for the first time, as the great silver snakes vanished, nothing more than wisps of smoke. Austin watched the woman for many moments, but his expression no longer contained awe; it was instead full of pity.

"I do not wish to train anymore." Austin's voice was strong. The Force's eyes narrowed to mere slits.

"What?" The voice was a low hiss; Austin recoiled in fright.

"Where is the spellbook?" Austin looked the Force in the eyes, attempting to stand his ground.

"I have hidden it."

"I don't want your powers anymore!" Austin's voice raised several pitches as he grew angry.

"My powers have done you nothing but good!" The woman pulled her hand back and Austin went flying over the crystals. He fell through the air, face first, and held out his hands to stop himself from hitting the crystals. The pain never came. Opening his eyes, Austin saw that he was hovering dangerously close to the crystals on the floor. Their sharp spikes glimmered at him like the teeth of some enormous beast.

"See what my powers can do? They can save you from pain, and possibly even death."

"But they can't bring others back to life," Austin found himself saying quietly.

"What did you say?" The woman came up to Austin, and lifted his head with her hand. Her black eyes bore into his own, but Austin could not feel the power transferring to him. The white hot pain of power entering his body was gone...all he could feel was the deep love for his father. Tears began to roll down Austin's face.

"I miss you so much," he sobbed to his father. "Father, please...come back."

"Stop crying...you fool! Your father died to save you, and all you can do is sob for him to return. Lift your head up, Austin, and look around. You are strong and power-ful...Everything your father would have wanted you to be. Now, accept my power!"

"This was not what my father would have wanted me to be. He wanted me to be honest and kind...success would follow, he always said. We have killed so many people...how could I have ever done that?" Austin's shoulders shook with tears. He closed his eyes once more. He felt the ground rumble underneath him once more, but kept his eyes slightly closed. When he opened them, he was hunched over on the floor in a secret room within the castle. Standing up slowly, Austin looked around him. There was no one there.

"Where are you?" He turned around slowly; he knew the Force would not have left so soon.

Hands emerged out of thin air, grabbing at Austin's neck. He gasped for air, and struggled.

The Force materialized, and whispered, "You are dead to me." Austin prayed as the stranglehold tightened. The Force leaned in so close to Austin that he could see the woman's perfect teeth.

"Prepare to join your father, Austin." The woman brought her hand back, and was about to strike Austin, when a voice echoed through the castle.

"Hello? Austin?" It was Tien.

The Force released Austin's neck, and vanished. He stood alone in the room for a moment, and then sank to his knees, sobbing quietly.

Chapter Twenty-Two

The Hidden Castle

It was not long before we had climbed the Steps of Death once more, and reentered the main hall. Ascending the stairs to the room where I had first seen the spellbook, we proceeded to examine the wall where Wise Woman had been.

"It looks like an ordinary wall to me," said Zharabi. Daya shook her head. "No, this is the entrance as I remember it."

"How do we get in?" I asked her. "Is there a password?"

"We have to make the door reveal itself," said Daya. Zharabi frowned, deep in thought.

"I think I can do it." Raising his right hand, he waited

while a ball of golden light appeared in the center of his palm. Pushing his hand forward, Zharabi propelled the golden light forward until it touched the wall, and was absorbed into the stone. For a moment, nothing happened. Then, slowly, a wooden door began to form from the stone. I waited until it had completely formed before grabbing the iron handle and yanking it open.

The room around us dissolved immediately, and we found ourselves in a garden behind the monastery. The hidden castle was in the center of the large garden, which was bordered by a hedge so thick that I could have walked upon it. Lining the hedge, and scattered across the rest of the garden were various statues, all of the same man. As we proceeded down the central path, towards the castle, I looked behind us, and saw a crumbling stone roof which had once sheltered a long walkway and well, both of which were now overgrown with weeds.

The noises had stopped now, and everything was silent around the monastery. The sun was beginning to set, and I shivered as we stopped on the threshold of the ancient castle. The stone was covered in moss and flowers, and the rotted door could barely stay on its hinges, but I could feel a deep sense of power from within the castle. Pushing the door open, I stepped inside, Daya and Zharabi behind me.

We were inside a modest entrance hall. It was swept clean, but there were no rugs on the cold stone floor. No lamps lit the dark hallway; our only source of light was the sun that filtered through the small dome-shaped windows at the sides of the hallway.

"Hello?" I called out uncertainly. There was no response, but I was sure that I had heard sniffling of some sort.

"It came from up there." Daya pointed to the stairs at the end of the hallway. I nodded. We continued slowly down the hall, taking our time to look into the deserted rooms on either side. All of them were as bare as the hall, none showing any signs of who had once lived here.

There was one final door left at the end of the hallway. It was near the stairs, and was shut tightly. Unlike the other rotted doors in the castle, this one was made of a dark blue marble. Silver-flecked stones glimmered from within the door, like eyes staring at me. I felt mesmerized by the glittering stone, and stepped toward it to open it. The door seemed to emanate the strong magical force that I had felt from within. It was locked tightly, but before I could touch the lock, Zharabi pulled me away, and pushed me towards the stairs.

"What?" My voice echoed through the hall. He pressed a finger to his lips for silence. As we climbed the stairs, he whispered into my ears, "That door holds great, danger-ous power. I could feel it within my veins."

We ascended the steps slowly, and I noticed that there were no windows in this area of the castle. Our path was lit by stubs of candles, which were held in place on the walls by crudely welded iron cups.

At the top of the stairs, there was another door. This one was already open, and swung slightly in the wind. Beyond the door, I could see a room that was once more lit by the fading rays of the sun.

"Is anyone here?" Zharabi pushed the door open slowly as he called out. There was no response, but I could have sworn I heard someone crying once more. I exchanged a look with Daya. She had heard the noise too. We waited in silence for a moment, but the castle seemed to be empty. Shrugging, Zharabi and Daya preceded me into the room.

It was unlike anything I had ever seen. Statues of different gods and goddesses that were nearly my height lined the room neatly, some made out of silver, others out of gold. Many glass cases lay scattered throughout the room, each holding an object of some value. Some of them were things that I had never seen or heard of before, things from a world unlike my own. Strangely enough, nothing was locked; I suspected that this was because Austin had never thought people would find this room, let alone dare to enter it.

My eyes were immediately drawn to a glass ball the size of my palm, filled with a silvery, swirling dust. Impulsively, I reached inside the glass case where it was housed, and shook the ball, and watched intently as the swirling dust receded to reveal a series of images.

There was a boy. He looked as though he were nine, maybe ten. He was on the floor, in shackles. Something was driving a silver beam of light into his heart, the way one would wield a sword. I watched as he writhed frantically, trying to escape from the force that held him prisoner. Unable to bear it, I shook the ball again, and another scene appeared. It was the same boy, except this time, he was at least thirteen. He was taller now, and looked evil. His eyes were black, and he laughed cruelly as he watched numerous silver balls fill with swirling white mist.

Before I could call Zharabi over, I heard a noise from behind me that caused me to turn abruptly. I waited a moment, still holding the glass ball in my hands. Then the noise came again, in the distance, but very clear. I could hear small sniffles, and rapid breathing. Walking past the many statues and other small prizes that were displayed throughout the room, I listened carefully for the noise as it grew slowly more audible.

At the end of the room, there was a blank stone wall. Putting my ear to the wall, I could hear someone crying beyond it. Holding the glass ball in one hand, I ran my free hand over the dark, flat expanse, looking for a hidden means of entry. To my surprise, I felt something irregular against the wall. It was an iron handle. Without thinking, I pulled at it.

The part of the wall that I was standing next to slid back. It was gone. Zharabi and Daya, who had been look-ing at the various statues, turned when they heard the grating of stone against stone. I found myself looking into a bare room, with the same yellowing stone as all the oth-ers. In the center of the room lay a figure shrouded by its black cape, shuddering as it attempted to quench its sobs.

Austin Chancellor looked up, shocked. I dropped the crystal ball. It fell to the floor, and shards of glass flew in all directions. I put my hands up, and ducked, just in time; one particularly large piece sailed directly past where my head had been only seconds earlier. Austin scrambled to the other end of the room, his hands over his head in weak defense.

Suddenly, images sprang from the remains of the glass ball, forming a transparent wall of constantly changing images between Austin and me. The vision I had seen of the boy and his father came first. I could sense Daya and Zharabi behind me as they watched.

As Austin's father lashed out at Daya's father with his long, silver blade, I heard her whimper behind me as the streaks of red blood ran through the tiger's coat like tiny rivers. Before I could turn to console her, another image had taken the place of her father's. Austin stood in front of the monastery, daunted by the building and the evil that emanated from it. He cautiously pushed the door open, and was almost immediately possessed. The Force encircled Austin, and a howling wind whipped around him. When it had died down, he looked the same—but his eyes were black.

Suddenly, Austin stepped over the glass on the floor, and the transparent wall vanished. He looked at me, and I backed away slowly from his gaze, but it was not like the ones I had seen before, cruel and calculating. Instead, Austin's eyes held fear within them. And although I believed it to be a trick of the light, his eyes appeared blue. Austin looked away quickly, ending the strange moment. When he turned back to me, his eyes were pitch black and hollow once more.

"What happened to your father?"

Austin placed his head in his hands for a moment, and I could hear his sobs. I gently placed the golden pocket watch on the floor. Austin slowly lifted his head to look at it. His eyes widened, and I saw them flash blue once more.

"Was that your father's?"

Austin nodded.

"Why didn't you fight the Force?" I was curious now. Austin lifted his head out of hands, and looked into the starlit sky.

Austin picked up the pocket watch, and clutched it as he spoke.

"I couldn't. I wasn't strong enough. And the Force had been like a parent to me…it gave me this home, with my father's treasures, and allowed me to control spirits. But ever since you arrived I've been remembering things that I had thought I'd forgotten…my childhood."

Looking up at me, after a long silence, Austin whispered, "You broke the spell….you broke the spell!"

I saw that his eyes were blue once more, and his hair had turned a light shade of brown. He had shrunk slightly, and we were the same height again. I smiled at him. He smiled back, and wiped stray tears from his face, then spoke with a renewed confidence.

"I wish I could take back the way my father died, and the way I did things…it was painful. I gained power, and it made me better, but the pain of losing my father never healed, even with all this time. I…" Austin faltered, but before he could say anything else, he was knocked down by Daya.

"How would you like to join him?" she asked angrily, as she leaned on top of Austin, her eyes glimmering.

"Daya, no!" I implored her, but she ignored me. Would we have come so far to free Austin only to have him killed now? My heart thudded, but I dared not stop Daya's terrifying rage.

"I had forgotten myself once more…you killed my father! I should never have come back to this battle… Struptha was right. It is not our battle."

A long silence followed her words. Daya continued to growl at Austin. He finally broke the silence in a surprisingly calm, quiet tone.

"I am sorry Daya. We have both suffered a similar loss. I know this cannot make us the same, but I understand your pain. My father did not mean to kill yours."

"It looked intentional to me," growled Daya.

"No. It was self-defense. There is nothing we can do to turn back time. You and I both know that. Please, let me go. Together we can fight the Force, and rid the mountains of this evil forever."

"Evil can never be eradicated," snarled Daya. "It can only be balanced. This seems like a good place to start." She raised her paw to strike Austin, who closed his eyes tightly.

"Daya, stop!" It was Zharabi who spoke now. Stepping forward, he pulled Daya off of Austin.

"What is wrong with you? Don't you want to revenge yourself on the one who made our lives living hell?"

"It wasn't him, it was the Force. Look at him, Daya. He is not a magical creature, and therefore not the true wielder of this power! We are fighting the wrong evil."

Daya said angrily, "If he is so inconsequential, then we should kill him now and be done with it!" She advanced towards Austin, but once again Zharabi stopped her. She turned to him and said in a low, threatening voice, "Touch me one more time, and you will pay."

"You cannot kill Austin. He is not the evil we have to fight."

Daya's muscles tensed, and she and Zharabi stood facing each other. I stepped between them and said angrily, "We only have a few hours until the sun and moon unite. If we cannot find the spellbook before then, we will all be destroyed, and the chaos Struptha spoke of will be absolute!"

Daya nodded curtly and turned to Austin, who sat on the floor, still looking slightly dazed.

"Where is the spellbook?"

"I don't know where it is. I don't know if you felt the rumbling, but the Force fought with me, and took the book from me. It is probably hidden in the garden some-where, but we must be careful, because in the monastery, the Force's power is rampant. It was once my power, but I think I am human again."

Turning to me, Austin smiled—a real smile—for the first time.

"You were right, Tien. I was never meant to be magical."

Zharabi said quietly, "Test to see if you have lost your power."

Austin lifted his hand into the air, his eyes focused intensely. Bringing his hand down, he murmured an incantation. Nothing happened. All of us were still as Austin tried twice more. Finally, Daya and Zharabi nodded. Austin gave them a wry smile.

"Fool," hissed a voice from the corner of the room.

We all turned slowly, and saw the Force shimmering behind us.

Chapter Twenty-Three

Stories Pieced Together

Spinning, the Force shifted into the shape of a young woman. Her hair was long and wavy, and cascaded down to her shoulders. She wore a flowing silver cloak that draped around her body, glowing with a strange light.

"How nice of you to join us." Zharabi smiled in an almost welcoming manner. The Force sneered in response.

"I was referring to you, dear Zharabi, when I called you a fool. Why didn't you say something? You knew I was here."

"What good would have come of it?" Zharabi stood his ground as the Force advanced slowly towards him. I backed away slowly, until I was in the corner of the room. Daya and Austin followed suit.

The Force continued speaking as though Zharabi had never asked the question.

"You were a fool to return to your original form, you were a fool to give your heart away. All along, I had always hoped that you would join me…"

"Something you knew would never happen!" Zharabi's voice was sharp for the first time since I had met him.

"You broke the rules! You, Zharabi, were once a human, something that no other shapeshifter could have ever been. Why would you choose to give up your shape-shifting powers for love?"

Silence continued to ring throughout the room. Out of the corner of my eye, I saw Austin slowly moving his hand inside his cape. I could see the glimmer of a blade, and tightened my grip on my own sword.

"Answer me! Why did you not join me? Together we could have been powerful. With the spellbook we would have created a dominion for ourselves stretching far across foreign lands!"

"I do not want immortality." Zharabi's voice was very quiet, almost a whisper. His face remained impassive as he spoke, but his eyes flickered with the faintest hint of anger.

"Then why do you want the spellbook?" The woman's face stretched into a sneer.

"I want to return it to the family it belongs to, and bring them back to life."

"Their time has ended." The Force said this with such finality that Zharabi shot back angrily, "You ended their time for them. No one should have that happen to them. Where is the spellbook?"

"Anger, anger." The woman gave a resounding laugh. "I was under the impression you were very even tempered, Zharabi. Why so touchy all of a sudden? Has your true past made you doubt your powers?"

Zharabi's eyes flicked quickly to Austin, then back to the Force.

"No, I..."

But what Zharabi was to say I never found out, for Austin leapt up, and rushed at the Force, brandishing his dagger.

Chapter Twenty-Four

In the Garden

The Force turned around quickly, and shot a bolt of electricity at Austin. He dodged it, and swung his dagger dangerously close to the woman's hand—only she wasn't a woman anymore. The Force had shapeshifted into a large python, which hissed at Austin, and bared its fangs. Zharabi turned to Daya, and nodded. She ran from the room, with me at her side.

"Tien, you have to go and search for the spellbook." Daya led me to the stairs. The Force ran out of the room after us, a woman once more.

"You!" Pointing a finger at me, the Force drew back its hand, and I could feel the ground shake under my feet.

"Tien, go!" Zharabi looked at me frantically as he created a force field with his hands to stop the Force's magic. Without looking back, I ran down the stairs, two at a time, nearly falling twice.

There was a loud bang from the top of the stairs, and I turned around just in time to see the steps crumble to a fine dust behind me. The tower was now precariously tottering. I was running out of time.

As soon as I scrambled out of the castle into the garden, I realized I had no idea where to look for the spellbook.

Suddenly, the ground rumbled again, shaking dust from the castle walls. I held onto the nearest hedge, and looked toward the castle. Through the windows, I could see Zharabi, holding back the Force's power with his bare hands, his face twisted into a grimace.

Letting go of the hedge, I ran through the garden, pushing aside the overgrowth, and looking behind the various statues that were scattered throughout the garden. Light had slowly begun to fade from the sky; I grew worried, for soon I would not be able to continue my search.

After several minutes, however, it was clear to me that there was no spellbook in the garden. I looked around, perplexed as to where it could have been hidden. My eyes fell on an old well overshadowed by the looming monastery behind it.

Running over to the well, I looked into its black depths. I couldn't see what was at the bottom, but I had a feeling that the spellbook had been hidden underneath the mask of the dark water.

Before I could pull the rope of the well up, however, a huge explosion caused me to turn around. Behind me, the tower of the castle had fallen in, and was now crumbling away from the building. A brilliant flash of silver light glowed through the gaps in the rocks, and I felt my heart beat faster as the Force rose from the tower as a shimmering mist. Once in the air, it transformed into a large dragon, bigger than the monastery. Its new shadow covered the entire garden, blocking out all chances of sunlight. I stood, frozen with horror, and watched as the dragon slowly beat its large, scaly wings once, twice, and then a third time.

The massive claws hung loosely in the air as the dragon soared over the garden, looking for something: me. I shrunk back against the wall, and felt fear turn my heart ice cold. Where were Zharabi, Daya, and Austin? I scanned the rubble-strewn garden, and knew that my only chance of getting help was to search the massive piles of rock that had once been the castle walls.

The dragon soared away from the monastery, and into the distance. I took my chance. Sprinting in the fading sunlight, I rushed to the rocks, and began to pick my way through the mess.

"Zharabi? Daya? Austin?" I dared not raise my voice above a whisper. A faint moan answered my calls from a few feet away. I followed the voice, and began to heave rocks out of my path. I soon could see Austin's face through the gap in the rocks. He was bleeding across his face, but seemed to be very much alive.

"Austin! What happened?"

"I was hit by the silver light the Force uses. It cut me across the face, but otherwise I'm fine. Here, help me." He handed me rocks, and I moved them away. Extending my hand, I helped Austin to stand. He looked haggard, and hurriedly wiped the blood off of his face, but seemed more worried as to where the Force had gone.

"It's changed into a dragon, hasn't it?" Austin looked at me grimly. I nodded.

"What does that mean?"

"A dragon is the Force's most powerful form…and now that I no longer have any powers, the Force has doubled its strength. What are we going to do?"

I shook my head.

"I don't know. Listen, do you think the Force would have hid the spellbook in the well?"

Austin's eyes lit up.

"Yes, of course! The well is enchanted. When you enter the water, the Force told me that you will be unable to come out alive. That seems like where the book would be. Only someone with power equal to that of the Force could enter the well."

"That would have to be Zharabi. We should find him." I felt my heart flip at the thought of Zharabi.

Austin was already looking among the nearest rocks, and whispering for Zharabi and Daya. I went in the opposite direction, looking for them as well. Suddenly, next to me, rocks shuddered and I saw a paw push one aside.

"Daya!" I forgot to lower my voice. Austin turned around and held a finger to his lips, his now blue eyes widening with fear.

Daya emerged slowly from the rocks and growled.

"Where is the Force?" She spat blood from her mouth.

"It went above the mountains. We think we know where the spellbook is; it's in the well."

"The Force will return. We should hide. Where's Zharabi?"

"I don't know. He isn't under the rocks, or we would have heard him."

Daya nodded grimly in response to Austin's statement.

"At the end of the fight, before the tower fell in, Zharabi let go of his force field. That could have been why the tower broke down. I don't know where he went after that, though."

"But how do we fight the Force without Zharabi?" I found that my heart was thudding loudly within my chest, a loud drum that rang in my ears. Where had the Force and Zharabi gone?

"He will be back. I think he is with the Force. We are wasting time." Before Daya could speak more, I heard a great cry come from the mountains. In the distance, I could see the giant dragon soaring back towards us, but it was no longer alone: upon its back rode Zharabi. Even as we watched, the dragon turned its head to spit fire at Zharabi. He leapt off of its back, and twirled through the air. I cried out, afraid he would hit the ground. As he fell gracefully through the air, Zharabi threw a golden thread at the Force, which looped around the dragon's claw. Zharabi held on tightly as the Force soared towards us, its mouth open in fury.

A jet of fire shot through the air, and nearly hit us. Just in time, Austin, Daya and I leapt out of the way. Rocks melted to a bubbling mass of slippery goo in front of my eyes. The fire burned high, and slowly began to spread across the other rocks, melting them one by one.

Running as fast as I could, I grabbed Austin and dragged him behind the nearest statue. We pressed ourselves tightly against the strong stone, listening to the dragon's heavy breathing as it landed.

"Where is the spellbook?" Zharabi could not keep the panic out of his voice.

The Force gave no response, but I could feel the earth shake as it walked to the other end of the garden. Zharabi remained where he was for a moment, and then lightly ran towards the hedge. Pushing back the brambles, he allowed Daya to exit. She looked murderous, and gave a low growl.

"Let me at the beast," she said in a voice of suppressed anger.

I watched as Daya crouched low to the ground, and picked her way around the remains of the castle towards the Force. The dragon's silver scales shimmered like armor against the light of the moon, which had now risen quite high in the sky. I saw its barbed tail disappear behind the ruin of the castle, and shivered.

A hand grabbed me from behind.

"Where is the spellbook?" Zharabi eyes traveled across my face as he whispered. I longed to speak with him, but instead pointed to the well. Austin murmured about the enchantment.

Zharabi shook his head.

"I am not the rightful owner of the spellbook. You are. I'll distract the Force, and you go to the well. Sangmu named you as the next Sorceress, Tien—you must do this."

I opened my mouth to protest, but Zharabi put a finger to his lips. I nodded, and peered out from behind the statue.

The dragon was at the far end of the garden now, searching the hedges for me. Daya was only a few feet away from the dangerous barbed tail, but she did not seem to be afraid of its menacing spikes. Silently, she ran several paces through the grass, before leaping off the ground.

In that split second that Daya traveled through the air, I saw the dragon turn its head, and when I saw its mouth open, I knew it was too late.

Before I knew what I was doing, I stepped out from behind the statue, and screamed "NO!"

The dragon turned its head, and I ran as the flames shot past me once more, the heat causing me to feel faint. I turned, and saw Daya land upon the dragon's back. Without hesitation, she sank her teeth into the hard, silver scales, and pulled one out viciously.

The dragon gave a roar that shook the earth. I ran towards the well, not looking back. Climbing up onto the edge of the well, I looked back once more at the dragon thrashing in the moonlight. As it threw Daya off its back, and she flew through the air, I saw Austin and Zharabi rush forward, Austin drawing his sword, and Zharabi slowing Daya's fall with his mystical powers.

Convinced my friends would not give up without a fight, I took a deep breath, and leapt into the black depths of the well, clutching my sword for dear life.

Chapter Twenty-Five

The Enchanted Well

As I fell through the air, there was no fear mixed with my emotions; I barely had time to think about what was happening before I was plunged into the cold, black water.

I opened my eyes almost immediately, and looked around me. I was still falling, through the endless blackness, as though the vortex would never end. On either side me, instead of the walls of the well, were strange silver snakes. They encircled me, but I was not afraid, for they did not move. Looking up, I saw the opening to the well glow red as flames enveloped it.

I finally fell out of the strange vortex that I had been a

part of, and closed my eyes tightly. I felt my body hit something sharp, but did not dare to open my eyes. Finally, I opened one eye, and saw that I had landed upon a silver crystal.

Where was I? Standing up, I found that I was in a dome-shaped room. It was very large, perhaps ten feet high. Looking around me, I saw only sharp silver crystals. I was surprised that I could stand on them, but soon forgot about that when I saw what lay beneath them.

The spellbook was trapped under the crystals, its worn binding slightly blurred by the walls of crystal protecting it. I placed my sword against the crystals, and hammered them, but only succeeded in creating loud echoes of the sonic clash between mineral and steel. Looking around, I wondered how to retrieve the spellbook.

"So you wish to retrieve the book?"

I raised my head at the sound of the new voice. At the end of the room materialized the ghostly form of a tiger. His coat shone silver, and the striped fur looked real enough to touch. When he walked across the floor, I noticed that his magnificent paws did not touch the sharp tips of the crystals; he glided as though he were flying.

"Yes. But I don't know how." I slowly stood so that my eyes were level with the tiger's. He smiled at me, his long, straight whiskers twitching slightly.

"It is not easy to retrieve the book. We were put here to protect it, should someone unworthy come to fetch it."

"We?" I looked around the room, but saw no one else. The tiger smiled, and indicated the area of the room behind me. Turning, I saw the shape of a tall, thin man forming from the same silvery material the tiger was made of. He smiled at me, and said, "Hello. I am the Ghostly Monk."

I nodded in respect, for the man was wearing robes inscribed with the same symbols I had seen on Sangmu's purple cloak so long ago.

"Who might you be?" The man was of Asian descent, and as he floated over to face the tiger, I saw stains of blood upon his hands. He chuckled when he saw my horrified glance.

"I was one of the original monks of the Ghost Monastery, as it is known these days."

"Oh...I see." I stepped away from the man. He laughed, the noise echoing around the crystal-filled room.

"No, we weren't violent at all! The monks were merely there to protect the abode of the king of the mountains." He inclined his head every so slightly to the tiger. I glanced at the tiger, and understood at once that this was Daya's father. At closer inspection, I could see that some of his stripes were indeed trails of blood upon his coat. The tiger nodded solemnly, and the monk continued to speak.

"For many years, we guarded this area of mountain. It was beautiful then! Flowers unimaginable to the common mind, trees with healing powers...they all grew here, in the castle of the great king. But then, Sangmu, our old friend, made a terrible mistake." The man's cheerful face grew grave here.

"She had been consumed with worry over her differences from others of her own kind. We advised her to not let her past hamper the future, but she would not listen. She created the Force," said the monk sadly.

The tiger continued the story now, his deep voice filling the cave.

"As we had feared, Sangmu soon could no longer control or stop the Force. She fled, and it came to the Monastery in order to conquer the heart of the magical kingdom here in the Himalayas. We put up a fight, but in the end, the Force trapped our souls, and we were subdued for all eternity."

"I don't understand," I said. "So you are here to guard the spellbook?"

"Yes," replied the monk. "We are here to stop those who come to retrieve it when it is not rightfully theirs. The Force would have us kill all who attempt to touch it…but you, my child, are different."

"The time has come for the sun and moon to unite," whispered the tiger in a hoarse voice. "We are mere hours away, young one. You must retrieve the book and rid the mountains of the terrible Force, or…"

"We will all be destroyed," I said quietly. The tiger and monk looked at each other, the back at me.

"So you have been to see the Dragon King," whispered the monk. "Then you are indeed the one to retrieve the book."

"What must I do?" I watched as the monk considered my question. Then, crossing his arms, he asked me, "Whom do you love more than anything in this world?"

I frowned, and closed my eyes as I tried to think. At

first, Wise Woman's face sprang to mind, but even as I opened my mouth, the monk said quietly, "No. She is not the one. Whom would you be willing to give your life for?"

Again, I was at a loss. The tiger said to me, "Love is the key to opening the spellbook. You must find love within your heart, and instead of casting it away as the creator of the spellbook did, you must use it to open the book."

"But I don't know!" I was growing frantic; time was running out. "I don't know who I would give my life for! My parents, I suppose, but…"

"No!" The monk exclaimed loudly, his robes billowing out as he rose higher above me. "Think again. Think more carefully…I have seen the face of the one you love, as has the king. How can you not have understood the power of love?"

Raising his transparent hands, the monk brought them down noiselessly. As he did so, an image of Zharabi appeared, floating in the air, his eyes wide with fear as he struggled to hold back the Force's magical power.

"Zharabi? I don't understand." My voice was suddenly emotionless as I attempted to comprehend what the monk told me.

My mind racing, I thought about Zharabi, and how he had shown me that love could come in many forms. I smiled through my tears, and felt my hands grow warm, as I thought of finding my parents, of Wise Woman's sacrifices for me…and of Zharabi, whom I had fallen deeply and truly in love with.

Looking at the monk, I saw that he was smiling. The tiger nodded at me, his whiskers once more curling as he bared his teeth in approval.

"At last," whispered the monk, "We may allow the true owner of the spellbook through to the dungeons to rescue those who are trapped."

"Thank you," I said quietly.

"May you destroy the Force for us all," rumbled the tiger. He stamped one of his paws upon the floor, and the crystals began to slowly dissolve before my eyes, as though they were nothing but figments of my imagination.

Chapter Twenty-Six

The Dungeon

When the crystals had completely vanished, I found myself standing in an empty room with no windows, and only one door that led back to the main hall of the Hidden Castle. I approached the door, but a dark stairwell caught my eye. I slowly climbed down it, my sword drawn, and the spellbook in one hand.

At the bottom of the staircase was a long room lit by black torches, and filled with silver cages. These varied in size based on what they held. As I walked through the room, I saw pure white unicorns with sparkling silver horns, dragons the size of small houses with their majestic heads bent low in despair. Fairies with sparkling wings of all colors stood sadly in their cages. All of them watched me carefully with wide eyes. I proceeded to the far end of the room, where a glass case as tall as the ceiling stood.

I studied the small boxes inside the display case. They were all identical and unmarked. Placing my sword on the floor, I slid back the glass door, and picked one of the boxes up. It was as heavy as lead, and I placed the minute wooden box on the floor. It trembled slightly, as though something within it was fighting to get out. Curious, I knelt down, and pulled the lid off the box.

White shapes flew out of the box immediately, soaring around the air and screaming with joy. Voices echoed around the room. I slowly stood up, and watched in amazement as the hundred or so spirits began to speak with one another.

"Excuse me," I said to the unicorn in the cage nearest to me, "but who are all of these people?"

"He can't speak. None of them can."

I jumped, and turned to see a spirit speaking to me. I asked the man, "Who are you?"

"We are the spirits who were killed before our time had passed, and captured inside that dreadful box…If someone is killed before their time, and it was not their destiny, the famed spellbook can bring them back to life. If not…they cannot be brought back to life."

The man's eyes widened when he saw the book in my hand.

"Please! Please save us from this fate," he said in a stricken tone, kneeling at my feet. "I cannot stay here much longer...I wish to return to my life as it was before I was taken from my family...my home."

"I cannot open the book!" I was distressed to see the spirit so upset. He looked at me, his eyes filled with translucent tears.

"Then you must destroy the great beast above us," he whispered.

I nodded. A resounding roar shook the ground. I was tempted to open yet another door at the end of the long room, but a shout from Austin stopped me. Snatching my sword up, I turned and ran away from the spirit, back past the magical creatures, and up the stairs to rejoin the battle. The spellbook remained tightly clutched in my hand.

Chapter Twenty-Seven

Austin's Redemption

As Tien leapt into the well, Austin rushed forward, his sword drawn. Dodging Daya's soaring body, he ran around the molten river of melted rocks to meet the dragon.

The Force's head wove through the air as it watched him carefully. Austin felt fear rush through his body, but instead of freezing him as it had done in the past, it gave him the strength to raise his sword against the powerful Force that had trapped him for so long.

"Austin, you fool! Put your sword down," cackled the dragon.

Austin shook his head. "I am not afraid of you any more."

The dragon roared with laughter.

"Look around you, Chancellor. How can you not fear such power?"

Austin did not respond, but looked behind him. Daya lay still in the middle of the melted rock. Zharabi had already reached her, and was carefully moving her away from the battle. Turning back to face the Force, Austin shook his head.

"You have killed so many for your own personal gain. Someone like you could never make proper use of the spellbook, because it was not meant for evil."

The Force rolled its eyes in an irritated manner.

"And how would you happen to know whether the book was made for evil or good? All that matters is who possesses it when the sun and moon unite. And when I succeed in opening the spellbook, I will have control of the mountains, and perhaps the land beyond it for all eternity!"

"You will be alone." Austin found that he felt pity for the Force, because it seemed to be friendless, and lonely.

"Friends are useless," hissed the Force. "Friends cannot give you power or strength."

"No, but they can protect you," whispered Austin quietly.

Holding out his sword, he rushed under the dragon's legs. Plunging his sword into the silver scales, he felt a vicious pleasure as the silver blood spurted out onto the grass.

Daya woke as Zharabi slowly pulled her out of the

rocks. Lifting her head, she slowly began to regain awareness.

"Where did Tien go?"

"Into the well."

Daya stood up quickly, her wounds still bleeding. As the dragon roared, and attempted to attack Austin, Daya ran, and sank her teeth into the other leg of the dragon. It howled in pain, and thrashed around, shaking the earth with every stamp of its massive leg. Daya quickly let go, and took shelter under the Force's belly along with Austin. Zharabi drew his hands back, and slowly released a thin golden thread, which snaked through the air, and circled the Force. The dragon watched the golden thread warily, distracted for the moment. Austin took this chance to creep out from under the dragon. Grabbing a scale, he pulled himself up onto the back of the beast. The dragon turned its head, and opened its mouth to breathe fire. Zharabi snapped his fingers, and the golden thread closed tightly around the beast's mouth. Zharabi kept his fist clenched as he attempted to hold the jaws of the dragon shut.

Austin wasted no time in bringing his sword down into the back of the dragon. Howling in mad pain, the dragon swung its barbed tail around, the spikes swinging dangerously close to Austin's right arm. He spun away from them gracefully, and was about to swing his sword into the dragon's neck, when the golden thread snapped.

"No!" Zharabi's fist unclenched, and he frantically drew his hands back again, but the attempt was futile. The dragon opened its jaws wide. Austin saw the forked tongue, and long, pointy teeth glow as fire began to rush up from the back of the beast's throat. Leaping off the Force's back, Austin landed hard on the ground, and picked himself up quickly. As his head spun, he could see the golden thread wind itself tightly around the Force's mouth as flames escaped the dragon's mouth. They shot by Austin, and landed on the grass, starting a fire.

Daya, who had been hiding under the Force, sank her teeth into yet another scale, and ripped it out. She was soon covered in the silver blood that already coated the grass. Spitting out the scale from her mouth, Daya growled.

Zharabi's face contorted with the effort of keeping the gold thread intact. The Force's jaws strained against the power of the thread that held his mouth closed.

Daya crept out from under the Force, and ran towards Zharabi. She watched as Austin came forward, his sword at the ready. Looking at Zharabi, she said quietly, "Austin's time is drawing close."

Zharabi nodded grimly.

Chapter Twenty-Eight

A Promise

As I pushed aside rocks to emerge from the ruins of the castle, night surrounded me once more, and I saw the battlefield from my position on the crumbling steps.

I cried out, "I did it! I have the spellbook!"

The dragon swiveled to look at me, its yellow eyes bulging with rage. It saw the spellbook in my hands, and looked at the castle. Sure enough, it had crumbled, leaving only rubble where the Force's room of power had once been. As I scanned the rubble beneath me, a loud noise from behind me made me jump.

The well had exploded. Water flew high into the air, a thick stream of silver and black shooting into the star-spattered sky. The silver snakes exploded into the air, leaving nothing in their wake. I was surprised at what had happened. Austin turned to look at me, smiling.

"You did it Tien! You got the spellbook!"

Before I could respond to him, the Force breathed flames. Austin leapt out the way, but not in time. The flames engulfed him, and for a moment, I could not see him. When they had died away, he lay still on the ground, his hands spread out across the grass. The dragon lumbered towards Austin. Daya leapt in its path, her ears pinned back and her white teeth revealed in a ferocious snarl. Zharabi joined her, his face showing anger for the first time. The dragon faltered, and backed away as Zharabi held up his hands, creating a golden forcefield. I ran down the steps, and sat next to Austin on the grass. His face and arms were burned dark black. He slowly opened his eyes, and winced. His hair was nearly completely burned off.

"Austin, I'm so sorry," I said quietly. He looked at me, his eyes blank for the first time since I had met him.

"I won't last much longer," he whispered to me. "Listen, Tien—there's one thing I thought you should know. These statues were of my father. I made them with the Force's magic, so that I wouldn't ever forget him. When you open the spellbook...I...I want you to bring my father back to life."

My eyes filled with tears as I saw Austin's hopeful eyes, despite his plight. He whispered, "Please, promise me you will bring my father back to life. He is somewhere within the monastery." A tear fell from one of Austin's brilliantly blue eyes.

I nodded, wiping away my own tears.

"I will bring your father back to life."

Austin nodded, and took a shuddering breath.

"Tell him I loved him..." Another rattling breath shook Austin's body, and then he stopped moving. His eyes remained open, but were now lifeless as they looked up at the moon. I gently touched Austin's hand, and whispered, "Don't worry, Austin. I won't break my promise."

Chapter Twenty-Nine

The Final Sacrifice

Standing up, I saw that Zharabi was growing weaker from holding back the Force. His hands quivered slightly as he pushed them forwards, driving the dragon back a few more inches. I felt anger well up within me as I saw the dragon leer at my friends. I turned to face the hedge. Hooking my hands securely around two of the many vines that crisscrossed to make up the hedge, I pulled myself up. My feet dangled in midair for a moment; the hedge shook violently. Without hesitation, I hauled my body up onto the hedge, and scrambled up.

Waving my arms wildly, I shouted, "Over here!"

The dragon saw me, and its eyes narrowed angrily.

With tremendous speed, it moved towards me, its nostrils smoking ominously. I was frozen. Where could I go?

I looked at the Force, and realized what it was about to do, almost too late. Opening its mouth, the Force breathed fire once more, lighting up the garden in an orange glow.

I turned, and began to run lightly along the hedge, my feet leaving impressions in the leaves. There was a loud explosion, and the hedge behind me burst into flames. I stopped short, and turned around to see the fire spreading. Vines fell limply to the ground, charred.

Only one thought filled my mind as I watched the fire devour the hedge: run. I began to sprint full out. The beast fired another jet of flames at the hedge. It missed me by less than a second. My heart was beating fast. Once the hedge was destroyed, I had no way out. I needed a plan.

My sword was still at my side. My hand crept towards it as another part of the hedge exploded behind me. Running as fast as I could, I drew my sword, and in the next moment, leapt off the hedge as the final shot from the Force blackened the remaining leaves.

I spun through the air, and landed on the back of the dragon. Turning, the beast did not hesitate to breathe again—but this time, silver electricity escaped the dragon's mouth. I held out my sword, and fell to my knees as my sword absorbed the jolt. As the dragon stopped exhaling silver electricity, I stumbled back, panting from the effort. The dragon swung its barbed tail, and I felt the spikes pierce my right arm. I cried out, and dropped my blade onto the grass below. I clutched the spellbook as tightly as I could, and forced my wounded arm to cling to the giant claw of the silver dragon.

Daya and Zharabi were upon the steps now, shouting to try and distract the Force. The dragon's eyes flicked towards them for a moment, then glowed with annoyance as Zharabi released yet another golden thread into the air. The Force snapped its jaws, but the thread nimbly moved aside. The dragon snapped uselessly at the golden thread, which taunted it mercilessly. Before I could leap off the back of the dragon, I felt its muscular wings beat as it rose into the air. I stood up quickly on the dragon, and viciously yanked a scale the size of my palm out of its skin.

We must have been at least twenty feet above the garden now—the stars were much closer from this distance. As I looked at the sparkling scale in my hand, the dragon roared in fury, and thrashed in midair. Looking in the sky, I saw that the sun was rising, but that the moon was not waning. It was nearly time for the sun and moon to reunite.

As I glanced down at the dragon beneath me, the shell that hung around my neck suddenly reminded me of Struptha's promise to come and help if he were still alive. Fumbling with the shell, I put it to my mouth, and blew as hard as I could. A single note echoed through the mountains. The dragon roared at the sound of the call for magical creatures, and thrashed back and forth angrily.

I jumped out of the way as the dragon turned, and snapped at me, its teeth glistening in the final rays of moonlight. Rolling off the back of the dragon, I held onto one of its claws, and dangled precariously in midair as the beast thrashed in pain. My right arm now hung uselessly by my side, and I felt the muscles in my left arm begin to grow tired as I was swung back and forth like a rag doll while continuing to clutch the spellbook. Raising my right arm, I ignored the immense pain and lifted the shell to my mouth a second time. The same note echoed through the mountains, and in the distance, I saw the large, hulking form of a dragon soaring through the air. Struptha was coming.

Beneath me, I saw the sparkling gold horn of a unicorn as he galloped into the garden. On his back rode a beautiful fairy, her golden-yellow hair glowing in the combined light from the sun and moon. She held a wand in her hand, and had large, glittering wings.

Struptha was very close now. He roared, "Let go of the dragon!" I closed my eyes, and obeyed him. As I fell through the air, I opened my eyes in time to see Struptha breathe red-orange flames at the Force. For a moment, the silver dragon was enveloped in flames, and it screamed horribly. Then, suddenly, silver electricity crackled from the center of the inferno, and Struptha was illuminated. He fell from the sky, landing heavily on the ground.

I felt my right arm go numb as I hit the ground. The spellbook slipped from my grasp, and the smell of burnt grass met my nostrils. I shuddered. Closing my eyes, I remained still.

Zharabi and Daya ran to Tien, but the unicorn bellowed, "Stay where you are!"

Bending his head, he whinnied and shot jets of sparkling, sunshine-yellow light towards the large silver dragon, who rolled around in midair, the silver scales falling like raindrops from its body. The eyes of the dragon roved across the ground until it spotted the unicorn. It breathed flames, and the unicorn pranced aside just in time: the grass beside him burst into flame. The fairy hovered beside him, then, raised her wand and allowed jets of blue light to shower the silver dragon. It turned on her, and seemed about to breathe flames once more, but she and the unicorn were ready.

The fairy placed her wand on the unicorn's horn, and closed her eyes, concentrating.

"Now!" she shouted. The unicorn bent his head, and a large stream of blue and yellow light left the unicorn's horn. He staggered back for a moment, but the fairy remained utterly still, her jaw clenched with the effort of holding the horn. The silver dragon was surrounded with the light for several seconds, and it appeared to be paralyzed. Finally, the unicorn raised his head, and the fairy dropped her wand to the ground. They moved over to where Struptha lay, his ragged breathing sounding loud.

The body of the great dragon hit the ground with a resounding bang, followed by the splattering of silver blood. Tien lay on the ground, mere feet from the Force. She slowly lifted her head, and struggled to reach her blade. Zharabi and Daya ran down the steps to come to the aid of their injured friend, but hesitated when they saw one of the dragon's large yellow eyes open.

The dragon looked blearily around, and then saw Tien struggling to grasp her sword. She did not look back at the Force, but merely gritted her teeth as her hand wrapped tightly around the tip of her blade. She stopped with a soft moan of pain.

Zharabi watched as the beast opened its mouth for one final burst of electricity—and he knew what he must do. Running forward, Zharabi launched his body nimbly into the air. As he soared into the path of the Force's electricity, Zharabi used his hands one final time to create a shimmering golden force field. His face contorted as the electricity hit him. His hands unfolded, and the golden wall began to fade.

Tien sat up, and hurled the blade at the dragon. It hit the beast square in the heart. The dragon stood up, and staggered several paces, but not before the electricity from the Force's mouth had enveloped Zharabi. As he fell to the ground, unmoving, the sun rose fully in the sky, next to the pale, round moon. The unity was complete at last.

Tien seized the spellbook. The dragon took a single step towards Tien, and began to roar in anger, but was cut off as its body began to vanish. The wind blew wildly as the dragon was carried into the air, and exploded into a thousand tiny fragments. These fragments were silver, like the blood and magic of the Force, landing all over the yard, and melting away into the grass.

As they did so, the silver blood vanished, and the hidden castle was rebuilt before Tien and Daya's eyes, several times more beautiful than before. The yellowing stone was now a dark gray, and vines grew all over the castle walls. The rotted door was now shining and new—the windows of the castle no longer held dark secrets behind them, and were illumined by panes of stained glass.

The statues of the man were next to go. They were lifted into the air, and exploded into fragments, which fell upon the burnt hedges and grass.

The hedges in the garden grew, and birds came over the mountains, landing on the light green leaves, chirping cheerfully to one another. The pathway leading out of the garden was well paved now, and the smell of wisteria floated through the air, sweet and lulling.

Tien and Daya turned as the monastery exploded. The rocks were lifted into the air, and vanished, just as the dragon had done, before exploding into tiny fragments that were carried away by the wind. After the explosion, grass and various flowers grew where the monastery had been, covering all traces of the Force's power that had ever existed.

From beneath the Hidden Castle came a rumble, and in the next second, spirits, closely followed by unicorns, fairies, and dragons, rushed out of the front doors, exclaiming at the sight of the mountains and talking amongst themselves.

The unicorn and fairy bent low over Struptha, speaking in low voices. A brilliant flash of blue light, followed by a jet of sparkling yellow light, hid Struptha from view. When the light faded, the fairy and unicorn backed away, and Struptha rose.

He bowed his large head to the fairy and unicorn before rejoining his subjects joyfully. The unicorn bowed to the fairy before trotting off to join the others of his own kind. The fairy waved happily to her subjects, and fluttered over to join them, hailed with cheers and shouts of joy.

No one took any notice of Tien, Daya, or Zharabi.

Tien crawled over to Zharabi, still holding the tightly bound spellbook.

"Zharabi?"

"Tien…I'm sorry."

"No, don't be sorry. You made the greatest sacrifice."

"If only I could stay…"

"You will stay! Daya is here too, you know. We can help you."

Zharabi turned his face to Daya, who smiled at him.

"You did well, Zharabi. You did well." Tears appeared in the deep amber eyes. Zharabi smiled, and said in a slightly constricted voice, "I only did what I felt was right. Tien…" He struggled to speak now.

"Yes?" Tien looked into Zharabi's eyes.

"Bring the spirits back to life, please." He closed his eyes.

"Wait! Please, don't leave me. I…I love you." Tien pleaded to Zharabi.

"I love you too, Tien," he whispered. Then, closing his eyes, his hand went limp.

Closing her eyes, Tien felt tears roll down her cheeks. Daya's head pressed against her shoulder gently, and Tien knew her friend was weeping as well.

Tien felt the spellbook leave her hands. As she turned to look at it, the bindings upon it vanished, and the book fell open on the grass. Tien opened the spellbook.

Looking at Daya, Tien said quietly, "I did it."

"Yes. The key was true—" Daya's voice faltered, and Tien finished her sentence.

"Love. True love. Like my mother's love for Li Shen… and my love for…" Tien could not finish the sentence, and speak Zharabi's name.

Turning around slowly, Tien saw the millions of spirits. Taking a deep breath, she opened the spellbook until she reached the incantation she was looking for. Raising her head, Tien slowly chanted the spell that would bring the spirits back to life.

Chapter Thirty

Joy Within Sadness

As Tien chanted, the spirits were slowly brought back down to the ground, and started to regain their human forms. The spirits began to leave the newly formed valley, and soon many forms had vanished down the various mountain paths.

"You used the necklace I gave you well." Tien turned to see Struptha standing behind her, the unicorn and fairy on either side of him.

"Thank you for giving it to me."

The fairy stepped forward now, her hazel eyes shining as she smiled at Tien.

"My name is Froalis, Queen of Fairies. You are very

much like Sangmu. She chose well."

"How did you know Sangmu?"

The unicorn whinnied, and said, "She made it a point to meet with the rulers of every kingdom within the mountains. I assume you will do the same." He held out a golden hoof to Tien. She shook it. "My name is Sunstream," he said, "and I am the King of Unicorns."

"We wanted to personally meet with you to thank you," Struptha said. "But wait...where is the golden snow leopard queen?"

"Over there." Sunstream indicated Zharabi's body, and Tien saw Daya sitting by it.

"She's the princess?"

"This is her castle," said Froalis. "She is the leader we all look to. It is up to the Sorceress and Ruler to preside over the mountains." She pointed at Tien, and waved her wand. Tien's clothing changed to long green robes, similar to the ones she had seen Sangmu wear so long ago in the village.

"Thank you."

There was a long silence after this, finally broken by Daya.

"Hello. Sunstream, Struptha, Froalis." She inclined her head to each of them in turn. Sunstream smiled at her, his golden mane rippling in the sunlight.

"You finally have your castle back. Congratulations, Daya."

Sunstream turned to look at the gathering of unicorns waiting at the other end of the garden. He said to us, "I will take your leave now, as soon as we complete the ceremony."

The other three nodded. Tien's heart beat faster as Sunstream approached her, his head raised proudly. Placing his horn on her left shoulder, he said quietly, "You have the support of the unicorns, Sorceress."

Then, without a backwards glance, he galloped to his herd. They whinnied, and he led them out of the garden, down the mountain path, and out of sight.

Froalis came forward next. Placing her hand on Tien's head, she whispered, "I pledge the fairies to help and support you throughout your reign, Sorceress." Then she, too, left the castle, flying into the sky with her companions. Tien watched them until they vanished behind the sun and moon.

Finally, Struptha approached Tien. Placing a large talon on her right shoulder, he said, "I promise to you, Sorceress, that the dragons you freed will come to your aid and cooperate with you during your reign." Lifting his claw from Tien's shoulder, he lumbered a few steps before his wings carried him into the air. The other dragons followed suit, and they flew south to the Dragon Pass, a dark blotch in the otherwise cloudless sky.

Daya turned to Tien, and said, "I will also take your leave now. We will be seeing each other soon, I expect." Instead of placing her paw on Tien's head, Daya stood on her hind legs, and placed her paws around Tien in a hug. Then Daya entered the Hidden Castle, closing the door behind her.

Tien turned to leave the garden when she saw a familiar man standing alone. His face was noble, and he seemed to be searching for someone. He wore simple British traveling clothes, and had the same blue eyes and brown hair as Austin.

He spotted Tien, and walked over. Extending his hand, he said, "Hello. I am looking for my son. He's about this tall, and has blue eyes and brown hair...Do you know where he could be?"

Tien said quietly, "Mr. Chancellor, I knew your son... unfortunately, he...has passed on."

"What? No! It couldn't be...he was only ten."

Tien turned and pointed to Austin's body in the distance.

"I'm sorry," she whispered, her voice shaking with sadness. "I-I knew him well. He said to tell you he loved you."

When this did not seem to improve Austin's father's spirits, Tien said, "If it helps, he died nobly, Mr. Chancellor. He saved my life."

The man wiped his tears, and lifted his son's body, carrying it down the hill and out of sight. Tien looked after him, a deep sadness filling her heart.

"He will move on. You have done your best."

"Wise Woman!" Tien ran to the arms of her guardian, who hugged her tightly, and said with a laugh, "I assume this means you got my note."

Tien nodded. When she attempted to smile, she faltered, and Wise Woman nodded knowingly.

"Look behind you." Tien turned to see the beautiful

garden and castle, Zharabi's body still lying in the shadows of the hedge.

"With great victory comes great loss, my child...this is something we must all come to accept in our time. For now, forget your sorrow...there are some people who are waiting to meet you."

"Who?"

Wise Woman only gestured. Tien looked behind her arm, and saw three people standing quietly in a row upon the grass. The first, a tall Chinese man, had lines upon his face, but otherwise looked happy. He held a sword in his belt, and wore armor on his body.

The next one was a young Indian woman. She too had lines of pain and anguish upon her face, but as her dark eyes returned Tien's gaze, Tien knew that she was no longer suffering. Her long black braid fell halfway down her back, a little longer than Tien's own.

Tien's gaze traveled to the final person in the row. He was old and stooped over, holding himself up with the help of a makeshift cane. His hair and moustache were white, and he wore simple threadbare garments. Despite his age and worn appearance, however, Tien had a strange feeling that this man was powerful.

"Do you recognize them?" Wise Woman murmured to Tien.

She smiled as Tien gasped—the individuals were her family: Li Shen, Rani, and Kamsa.

Chapter Thirty-One

The End Begins

"Mother? Father?" My voice cracked as I spoke. They nodded hesitantly, and opened their arms. I ran towards them, and they hugged me joyfully. As I breathed in, I smelled bamboo and jasmine, and, for the first time in my life, I felt as though I was truly at home.

I moved away to get a better look at the parents I had never known. My mother smiled, and said in a gentle voice, "We are so proud of you, Tien."

My father nodded in agreement. "You have become everything we hoped you to be…we are sorry we could not raise you."

"It doesn't matter now," I said with a smile.

"We are still a family. We will always be." My mother said these words with finality and strength. I turned to look at Wise Woman, who directed a meaningful gaze toward my grandfather. He was still looking at me gruffly. I let go of my parents, and they stepped back as I approached Kamsa.

"Grandfather...I believe this is yours." I held out the opened spellbook.

My grandfather took the book from me with open hands. He trembled as he flipped through spell after spell.

"You-you opened it." His voice was deep and rumbling, and reminded me of a rushing river.

"Yes," I said quietly.

He closed the spellbook carefully, and I remembered to pay my respects. I bent down, and touched Kamsa's feet. He touched my head, and gently allowed me to come back up. I faced him, and saw that he was closing the book.

"My actions ruined nearly everything. I am so sorry... Tien." He said my name nervously. I threw my arms around me, and he hugged me back. I whispered to him, "I love you, Grandfather."

He didn't respond, but the tears that rolled down his face were enough.

In the hours that passed, I sat with my family and spoke with them at length. It felt as though the years that had so cruelly separated me from them melted away with each time my mother stroked my head, with every time my father patted my shoulder. I learned of how my life would have been if I had grown up in the village with my grandfather and parents. Surprisingly, I was not as enamored with this possibility as I had been when I was young. My life now seemed to me exactly how I had always wanted it; I had finally found where I truly belonged.

It was this realization that led me to decline my family's offer to have me live with them. I understood that my true place was in the mountains, as the next Sorceress. Although I knew in the back of my mind that the time must come where I must part from my family, I prayed that they would be able to stay even another day.

As the sun's brightness dimmed, and the moon's silver sheen grew brighter, Wise Woman looked at me. She did not speak, but her face told me that it was time. I stood, and my mother and father mirrored me, their faces sad that our unity must end so soon.

Wise Woman led my parents and grandfather along the path to the valley, waving at me until they vanished. Lowering my hand, I turned to where Zharabi's body had been, and was shocked to find that it was gone. I realized that Daya had disappeared into the mountains with the other kings and queens who had so valiantly fought, and that I would never see her again. My heart seemed to quiver at the thought.

Feeling hollow and empty, I climbed high into the mountains alone, until I reached the grove, still on the highest peak of the tallest mountain. As I stepped over the protective wall of pure white marble, I felt a peace settle over me, and felt my soul rest for the first time since Austin's death. However, my heart still ached for Zharabi. Ignoring this feeling, I began to prepare for my penance, beginning another chapter of my life.

Epilogue

Reunited

It was a sunny morning, and Tien was tending to the neem tree. She looked sad, as though a bad memory had assaulted her from the past, although a fair amount of time had passed since she had defeated the evil Force. Tien's frail frame and tired, lined face revealed the sadness and pain that had haunted her for three long years.

A wind began to blow in the grove, ruffling Tien's hair, and causing the bamboo to swish to and fro, like weeds in a cornfield. The flowers of the neem tree swayed in time with the wind. Tien lifted her head, and for a moment, could almost seem younger, as though she was remembering a past which did not include sadness or pain...only happiness. She was carefree, and a shadow of a smile played around her lips. The wind died down, and Tien returned to her work, her back beginning to stoop again, and her face sinking back into sadness.

The bamboo trees rustled again, and Tien looked up.

"Hello?" Her voice was soft and almost lost in the mountains. The trees rustled one more time, and Tien took a hesitant step forward. The trees were pushed back, and a tall man stepped out.

His skin was mocha colored, and contrasted his dark eyes, which were intense. His hair was short, and ruffled in the wind that had begun to blow again. He was tall and agile, at least one head taller than Tien. He smiled at her, and his eyes seemed to light up as he did so. Tien put down her basket, and looked at the man carefully. Her mouth was open slightly, as though she couldn't believe what she was seeing.

"Zharabi?" Her voice was hoarse, and tears threatened to spill over from her eyes.

He nodded.

The age lines seemed to lift from Tien's face as she ran to him. He swept her up in his arms, and twirled her around in the air. Tien's youthful looks were returned. She smiled, and for the first time in many long years, laughed with joy. Zharabi carefully placed her on the ground. She put her hand to his cheek, and felt it gently, as though afraid he might disappear into thin air at any moment. Zharabi shook his head.

"I'm not going anywhere, Tien."

"What happened to you?" Tien's voice was returned all ready; her former beauty shone once more.

"I didn't die. You saved me, Tien. When you pledged your love for me...it prevailed over fate."

Tien blushed, and smiled.

"We opened the spellbook too. And the spirits...I freed them...my family is happy now...Austin's father buried him...the new age has finally begun."

There was a silence, as though Tien expected Zharabi to say more, but he did not speak. Turning from him, Tien began to walk back towards her basket, a strange sense of pain piercing her heart. She knew she had hoped for too much...Zharabi would not want to help her or return to the mountains.

"Wait! Tien!"

Zharabi called out, his voice confused.

"So what about me?"

Tien opened her mouth, and then closed it again.

"What do you mean?"

Zharabi shrugged as though this question was of little importance to him, but failed miserably.

"Well, I thought I might be able to help you..."

"Help me?"

"...to rule," said Zharabi.

A long silence elapsed, as Tien stared at Zharabi, surprised. He looked nervously back, awaiting her decision.

"Of course you can," said Tien quietly, breaking the silence.

Zharabi took the basket from Tien, and placed it on

the ground. He began to continue her work of picking neem flowers from the leafy tree. Tien joined him, and the two worked together in peace, completing their story, and binding their love forever.

Acknowledgments

The publishing of *Sorceress of the Himalayas* would not have been possible without the help of The Book Designers and their very talented and dedicated team.

Usana Shadday, who has been very patient in answering each and every question regarding the publishing process, and has given me valuable advice with not just the layout of the book but also with other aspects of the book-publishing business.

Ian Shimkoviak and Alan Hebel for their hard work, talent, and sensitivity in creating such a marvelous design and layout.

Scott Erwert for taking my vision of Tien Ming and bringing her to life with his fabulous illustrations. His attention to detail in each of the sketches in every chapter and on the cover truly makes the book come alive.

Mark Burstein, who has exhibited tremendous forbearance with all my "little" changes in the book even after it had been edited many times over.

And finally, I would like to acknowledge the two members of the WEP for all their support and encouragement for me and for my novel; my first editor and publisher are two dedicated people whose efforts I will never forget.

About the Author

A lifelong passion for reading and writing inspired Ketaki Shriram to write *Sorceress of the Himalayas* when she was thirteen years old. Her vivid imagination and mature skills produced an extraordinary tale. She is now a junior in high school and lives with her family in California.